ékleipsis

the abyss

TAMEL WINO

To the Musih Tedji Xavieres of the world — for the enlightenment, and for inspiring me to take the plunge.

First paperback edition October 2021

Book design & Illustrations by Nuno Moreira, NM DESIGN

ISBN 978-1-7774088-5-5 (paperback)

ISBN 978-1-7774088-4-8 (ebook)

www.ekleipsis.ca

"Deep into that darkness peering, long I stood
there, wondering, fearing, doubting, dreaming
dreams no mortal ever dared to dream before."

— Edgar Allan Poe

"And I, infinitesimal being, drunk with the great starry void, likeness, image of mystery, I felt myself a pure part of the abyss, I wheeled with the stars, my heart broke loose on the wind."

— Pablo Neruda

MARLENE

My finger is bleeding.

I clench my hand into a fist and jam it into my pocket to avoid looking at it. I've been trying so hard to grow out my nails, but last night the nerves got to me, and I ripped off the brand-new nail I've been cultivating on my right index finger. Damn it. I've been so good about it, and now two weeks' work is gone and I'm probably bleeding all over the inside of my blazer pocket. This would be bad enough on a normal day, but there's no way I can get through this interview with my dominant hand in my pocket, because I talk with my hands all the time. I'm great on paper—articulate, witty, critical. It's just when opening my mouth that I feel the need of something else to back me up, so I always end up using my hands to compensate. Maybe if I fail this interview, I can give up the writing career and become a mime instead.

There are three other people waiting with me. We exchange polite smiles. They are probably sizing me up as I am them, wondering what their resumes look like, what kind of bylines they're used to, if I know them from social media. Do they have that sparkle or talent that Damien Wolfenstein, the billionaire philanthropist, is looking for—the perfect writer to entrust with his life story?

Hopefully he's not looking for someone with a complete set of nails.

I drag my gaze from the waiting room door and instead stare out the window, which takes up almost the entire far wall and gives a very impressive view of the city skyline. The sky is blue and clear, and the sun sparkles on the buildings around us, glittering on concrete, steel, and glass. The waiting room itself is plainer than I expected from Damien Wolfenstein, who, from the articles and profile pieces I've read, gives the impression of spending a lot of time poised elegantly on a leather Chesterfield, emanating Tom Ford aftershave, writing fantastic anecdotes in a leather-bound journal with a Montblanc fountain pen. I thought at least the chairs in the waiting room would be expensive, but they look more like something you'd get from IKEA. Maybe he's stingy with his money. That wouldn't surprise me. Damien Wolfenstein would be the most high-profile client I've worked with, but I'm no stranger to publicly wealthy people being eye-wateringly tight with finances.

I once interviewed a famous model who refused to buy a drink and insisted that we both only have tap water. At some point, I sneaked in an order of a mojito on my way back from the ladies' room. As the drink was placed in front of me, she glanced at it, then did a double take. She was still sulking when we parted.

This waiting room is as uncomplicated as a Margherita pizza—plastic and wooden chairs flanking the walls, a nondescript beige carpet, a pine-veneer table, and a few bland, framed prints on the pale cream walls.

I peek at the wounded finger. It has stopped bleeding, but the corner of my painted white nail is stained.

The door opens, and I can't stop my head swinging around

like an excited puppy.

It's the tall, bored, elegant assistant who showed me in here. She calls, "Hazel Landis?" managing to make it sound like it's the dullest name she's ever heard.

I shoot to my feet, smoothing down my skirt. "Yes?"

She gestures, and I follow her out of the room, feeling the eyes of the other candidates burning a hole in my back. The secretary takes me down a corridor and stops in front of an unmarked door. "He's ready for you."

"Thank you." I touch my hair briefly and adjust my blazer. My finger stings. I knock on the door.

"Come in," says a voice from inside, and I enter the presence of Damien Wolfenstein.

I already know what he looks like, of course, but it's still a shock to see him in the flesh, standing up and leaning over his desk with his hand outstretched. His famous blue eyes are a little less striking in person, perhaps, but the salt-and-pepper hair is waved so perfectly, and the infamous smile is so dazzling, he might as well have just been cut out from a glossy magazine.

"Hazel"—that rich, silky-smooth cappuccino sound, so distinctive it makes me smile at the incongruity of it forming my name. "Thank you so much for coming in."

"Mr. Wolfenstein." I take his hand, shake it firmly, using the motion to recollect myself. I'm too seasoned for nerves, and this is just a job. Not even a job, it's an interview. Get a grip, Hazel.

"Please, call me Damien." He gestures to the chair in front of his desk and waits for me before he sits down again. He showcases sets of brilliant, white teeth in contrast to his lightly tanned face. I don't know if he uses sunbeds or if he just takes a lot of tropical holidays. He's wearing a neat white V-neck t-shirt, sleeves imprinted with the famous logo that I recognize from Gucci's latest collection, so that at least is more on brand for him than the waiting room. It shows off the glow of his skin, and the cut of it flatters his frame; he has the look of a man who takes care of himself with the kind of casualness you can only achieve with a dedicated team of stylists. He's in his fifties, but if it wasn't for his silver hair, he could easily look at least a decade younger.

"Damien. Thank you for seeing me today."

"Oh, not at all. The pleasure is all mine." He looks down at a folder on his desk. "Your resume is outstanding. I particularly enjoyed your article on the Fulton scandal. Very impressive."

"Thank you. That put me on the map."

He glances at me, and a corner of his mouth quirks up in a smile. "You practically ended his career."

I raise my eyebrows. "Fully deserved. Don't you think so?"

He laughs. "I do. I'm glad you're honest."

"Rather than modest?"

"Are they mutually exclusive?"

"When it comes to my bylines, yes. If I don't think I'm capable of doing a good job, why am I even here? I'd be wasting both our time."

"So, honesty is important to you."

"Most of the time."

"Only most?"

"Well, I am a writer."

"What kind of quantities are we talking about, with regards to honesty? Seventy-five percent honesty, eighty percent…"

"You're the client. I can be as honest as you want me to be."

"Or as dishonest?"

"Maybe that, too."

He leans back in his chair, smiling. I am too, but my heart is beating rather quickly. I like him. And this. Didn't expect myself to be quite so frank, but Damien seems like a man who appreciates this kind of tone.

As if reading my mind, he says, "You're the first interviewee to make me laugh. Which is a good sign. I want someone who'll bring a sense of humor to this project. Some of my life—well, it's been pretty ridiculous. I want someone who can capture that feeling of the absurd without turning it into satire."

I nod. "Do you have an outline ready?"

"Not yet. That's something I'd want to work on with you. I have a lot of ideas about what I want to include, and I need to whittle the list down. In my case, it may be a problem of too much material, not a lack of it."

"That's great, though, it's always better to cut things rather than pad them out unnecessarily."

"Oh yes, there'll be no padding needed. Some of it…" He hesitates a moment. "Some of it's pretty intense. I should warn you now."

I smile. "I'm good with intensity. The spicier the better."

He returns my smile, and I realize how that sounded, like I'm after sordid details of his playboy days. But I don't want to back down, and Damien doesn't seem offended.

"On that note," I say, "reliving the past and going back over old memories can be a very extreme experience for some people. I'm not doubting your ability to handle that, but it's something to be aware of."

He nods. "Thank you. Yes, I had thought of that. I'm sure we'll uncover some skeletons in due course." He laughs a little oddly and seems to be thinking about something for a moment. Then he shakes his head. "We'll cross that bridge when we come to it."

"Sure."

"Well. Hazel." Damien leans forward over the desk. "I've made a lot of great decisions based on first impressions. And I've got to say, you've made a fantastic first impression. If you want it, the job's yours."

I'm so surprised that for a moment I forget my words and just stare at him. Finally, I manage to reply, "That's wonderful! Thank you for the opportunity," and shake the hand he's holding out to me.

"I'll get Stephanie to email over the contract later today," Damien says. "And set up our first appointment together." He presses a button on his desk. It buzzes, and a moment later his secretary opens the door.

"Cancel the rest of the interview appointments and tell the other candidates they can go home," Damien tells her. "The position has been filled."

*   *   *

That night I cracked open a bottle of bourbon to celebrate. The following Monday, I'm walking along the same corridor to Damien's office. In his email Damien instructed me to come straight through, and the secretary gives me a bored, perfunctory smile as I walk past her.

Damien answers the door so quickly I wonder if he was

standing behind it, just anticipating my arrival. The idea of him waiting is strangely vulnerable, and I return his grin warmly. Today he's in another expensive t-shirt and black jeans. "Sit, sit," he says. "Tea? Coffee?"

"Coffee, please. Black, no sugar."

He goes to the fancy-looking espresso machine on the sideboard. I watch the muscles in his back move beneath his white shirt, the tanned line of his neck and the brush of silver hair against his nape. I'm not starstruck, but no one can judge me for admiring him from a distance.

Damien brings my coffee and puts it down on the desk in front of me. I wrap my fingers around the little white cup, feeling the warmth seeping through the expensive china, and smile at him. "How are you? Are you ready to show the world your true greatness?"

"Good. Good, yeah." He pauses and sits down on the opposite side of the desk. "Well. If we're being honest…" He flicks a look at me I can't quite read. "I'm nervous." This man had braved hostile expeditions through the Amazon, negotiated with some of the most powerful figures, and survived a war as a jet fighter pilot. Thinking that he's jittery about an interview with some journalist makes me chuckle inside. *Well, I'm not just some journalist, I'm an award-winning ... Stay focused!*

I nod. "That's understandable. It's quite an undertaking, laying out one's life in chapters and sentences. It can be hard, too, to present your experiences in a way that will make sense to a common reader. Demoralizing, sometimes."

"Demoralizing?"

"Yes. I had a client once, and it took so much for her to peel back the layers from her life. She was so private, and there were lots of events in her life that had profoundly affected her. And yet when she put them down on paper, they didn't look like much at all." I smile reassuringly. "But that's okay. It's my job to make sure people see those events and react to them so they see what you saw, feel what you felt."

"You mean, I had my heart broken when I was twenty-two but that's not enough? Heartbreaks are commonplace. Cliché."

"Kind of like that, yes. My job is to present your heartbreak as the reader's heartbreak so they can feel what you felt."

"You're going to get into my skin, then. My brain." Damien cocks his head at me. He's rolling a pen between his fingers. I want to look and see if it actually is a Montblanc fountain pen, but his eyes are arresting. It's not just their color, although the blue is so striking it almost seems artificial. There's an intensity there I can't draw away from. The kind of eyes a girl could get lost in. He gazes at me, and for a moment I forget what I was saying.

The whir of the AC unit coming back to life breaks our eye contact. My voice is cool, professional. "So, you had your heart broken when you were twenty-two?"

"Oh, yes." He laughs easily. "That and several other times."

"You sure it's not the other way? Heard you're quite the player."

He snickers. "Whatever you've heard, I can assure you that I'm a true gentleman."

I rummage in my bag and take out my little recorder and my laptop. "Do you mind if I write notes during this session? I'll be taping all of it, but I like to make notes as well, so I have something to cross-reference with the recording."

"No, not at all. You're very thorough."

I don't know what it is in his voice that manages to make

that sound like an innuendo. A strange, unexpected excitement suddenly quickens inside me. I glance up, and Damien's intense oceans of blue are back on me. I smirk, very aware of my mouth, of Damien looking at my lips.

"Tell me about them, then," I say, then immediately realize that it came out like a challenge. "Tell me about all the women who broke your heart."

*   *   *

"So, of all the lovers you've been with, is there one that you would consider the most special? The one that got away?" I uncross my legs, not taking my eyes off his. He's no longer sitting in his chair. His butt is perched on the edge of the desk, arms crossed.

I must admit, it's been an intriguing and entertaining session with Damien. He's been quite open about his past. His childhood, his humble beginning as a caddy, the successful career as an insurance agent, and the very first company he owned, a pharmaceutical enterprise. But surprisingly, he's rather coy when it comes to past relationships. This is the reason why I'm revisiting the topic at the very end.

He hesitates for a split second. "None, actually. Just like all my business models, when it comes to my love life, I learn from past mistakes and strive for improvements." He smirks. "Each is better and shinier than the last one."

Then he looks me up and down, mumbling, "Case in point."

I clear my throat, pretending not to hear his last comment. "Well, I think we're done here for today. Thank you for your time and invaluable commentary.

I scroll back through my notes and switch off my recorder. Damien watches me closely as I slide my laptop back into my bag.

"This was a good session," I say.

"Yes," he agrees. There's an undercurrent to his voice that makes me delay with my bag strap to hide the smile on my face. "I had a great time."

I manage to maintain control. I push back my hair and stand up from my chair. "Same time on Friday?" I say, offering my hand and trying to sound casual.

Damien uncrosses his arms, pushes himself away from the desk, and saunters in my direction. He stoops forward. He's so close that for a moment I think he's going to try and kiss me. His aftershave is potent, cedarwood and something sweet and citrusy, tingling in my nose and throat. "Have dinner with me," he says.

I raise my eyebrows. "The coffee is not doing it for you?"

"I'm serious, Hazel."

"So am I, Damien."

"I want to take you to dinner."

"That's very kind of you."

"Is that a yes?"

"It's not a no." The exhilaration rises in my stomach, and I can't stop the smile curling around my mouth. "Okay, sure. Friday?"

"Friday." Damien grins at me as he pulls away. His eyes are blue like gas fire, and there's a hunger in them that sends a tingle down my spine.

*   *   *

I'm surprised and a little embarrassed at how long it takes me to dress on Friday. I spend way too long standing in front of my mirror, holding up outfit after outfit to find the magical combination that will wow the billionaire style icon. I want to impress him but at the same time not make it too obvious.

Eventually I settle on a simple black pencil dress and my favorite fancy shoes—black suede ankle boots with bright gold buttons down the side. I pat on some red lipstick and have another moment of hesitation over what perfume to wear, deciding on my normal fragrance over anything higher-end, even though I know it comes from a perverse desire to show Damien that I'm not dressing up for him.

My appearance is satisfactory, and I give my reflection a brief nod as I head out of the door.

The car Damien had sent to pick me up drops me off at a restaurant near the harbor. I've never been in here before, but as soon as I step through the door and a waiter appears to take my coat and call me "madam," I can tell what level of establishment this is. The floor is rich shiny wood, glossy and bright under the light of dozens of softly glowing lamps. The windows are huge, overlooking the dark waters of the harbor. I spot an actress from the latest superhero franchise sitting at one of the tables, but the waiter guides me neatly through the restaurant to the corner where Damien is already waiting for me.

Damien looks up and sees me, and for a second his face takes on a peculiar expression I can't read—it can't be dismay?—but then it's gone and he's on his feet, pulling out my chair for me.

I sit down, and he says, "You look extremely beautiful."

I smile, "Likewise," and I gesture to his crisp white shirt and charcoal suit. The grey and white colors make his eyes startlingly bright. His skin glows with health, and when he puts his hand over mine, I don't object. He's smiling, but there's still a suggestion of something else behind his practiced ease—a hint of the emotion I glimpsed earlier. I don't look away, leaning in a little over the table, my elbow brushing the decanter of water and the cold, condensation-streaked glass sending goosebumps up my arms.

I flash him a smile, knowing that he'll read it as the challenge it's intended to be.

For a moment we hold it, both of us smiling, both of us silent, the air between us vibrating with all the things we're not saying to each other. Finally, Damien blinks. He leans back in his chair, and I unfold my napkin briskly to hide my triumph.

Damien Wolfenstein might be a billionaire, and a philanthropist, and an artist, and—if the rumors are to be believed—an ex-spy, but he craps and bleeds, just like everyone else.

He moves for the decanter, but I take it first and fill both our glasses. I take a sip of water, ice cubes against my teeth, and watch Damien over the rim of my glass. This time I can read his expression perfectly. Frustration.

"You didn't have to come here," he says.

"I wanted to come here," I say.

"Did you?"

"Yes."

"You're not acting like it."

"How should I be acting?"

"You should be letting me treat you right, for a start."

"And what does 'letting you treat me right' entail exactly?" I put down my glass, hearing the firm clunk of it against the table. "Or by 'treat me right' do you mean things like order my food for me, pour my water for me—"

"Back down in a staring contest?"

"Is that what it was?"

There's a moment of uncomfortable silence. I wonder if I blew it, if that was too far. He still is my client, after all, no matter his ideas on women. Damien looks down at his hands, still on the table. Then he shakes his head. He cackles. "Damn it." He looks up at me, face as bright as the moon. "Yes, I suppose so, it does mean all those things."

I smile. "You're old school, Damien. But that's okay."

"Oh, it is, is it? Thank you very much."

He laughs, ruffling a hand through his salty-grey hair. It makes him look younger, almost boyish, despite what I just said. I want him to take my hand again, to play the game and be the demure date dazzled by his wealth and class. But I'm not like that. And I never lie to my clients.

The waiter comes back. Damien orders steak, bloody and rare, and I order a mushroom pie with coconut cream, rosemary, and red wine.

"You're vegan?" Damien asks.

"I try," I say. "I'm not militant. But I like the idea of walking lightly upon the earth. Causing as little damage as I can while I'm here."

"I'd have thought you'd be more in favor of leaving a legacy."

"A legacy, yes. I want to make an impact, leave an impression of myself after I've died. I love that idea. That I could create something—write something—that people will be able to see years after I'm gone and get a sense of who I was."

"Immortality, of sorts."

I nod. "Yes, I suppose so."

"Isn't that a kind of damage, though? You're still affecting people's lives, years after you've gone. Instead, you're a ghost, haunting the people who should have moved on. Should have forgotten you."

I chortle to cover the sudden unease seeping through me. Damien plays with his glass, swirling the water around inside, and the act is so exaggeratedly casual that I'm not sure what I'm actually looking at. Damien's head is bent over. I can only see his forehead, smooth in a way that must be Botox but still looks natural, and the shadow of his sculpted cheekbone. It's like I'm looking at a glossy photo again, the crafted reality of magazines and Instagram feeds, not the skin-and-flesh reality of a human being.

"Actions always have consequences," he says softly. His voice, the movement of his hand with the glass, it all feels too staged. Something unreal. Like he wants me to ask further, dig and prod and find out what he's really talking about.

I shake my head and make myself laugh. It comes out too loudly, too abruptly. But it gives me a punctuation mark for the conversation to change direction. "And that's the theme of chapter seven," I giggle, picking up my glass, raising it into a toast.

For a moment Damien is still. Then, like flicking a switch, his face changes and the familiar smooth smile comes out again. He raises his glass and touches it to mine. "Chapter seven," he says.

Our food arrives quickly. It's every bit as amazing as the reviews say; the succulent, deliciously sautéed mushroom, and the sweet, crunchy avocado corn salad.

Damien seems to have recovered from his strange mood, too. His conversation sparkles like the water in his glass. After finishing his meal, he leans closer, his honeyed voice drizzling sweet melody into my ears. His fingers caress the smooth, ruby red tablecloth. Almost touching mine.

"Why did you invite me here?" I ask after he finishes an anecdote of the weekend he and Elon Musk spent together in Berlin.

"It's my favorite restaurant. My friend Marlene keeps her yacht here, so I come by quite regularly."

"That's not what I meant."

"I know it's not."

"Well, then."

"I want to get to know you a little better. And you me, hopefully." He grins, shining teeth and steady gaze. "Is that a crime?"

"Of course not."

"Not yet, anyway."

"Are you planning on creating any new skeletons for your closet, then?"

"No. Just thinking about the old ones."

"The scandalous details." I sip my wine. It tastes expensive, and the reality of where I am and who I'm with sinks into me, making me smile and soften. His eyes are intently watching the movements of my mouth, but that doesn't affect my lightening mood. "That's what I'm here for, Damien. I'm here for all of your dirty laundry."

"If you can handle it."

"Oh, I can handle it."

We leer at each other.

The meal finishes with mango sorbet and cocktails. As Damien helps me into my coat, he says, "What about a walk along the pier?"

I take his arm and we walk together into the cool night air.

Damien's arm is solid under my hand, and the warmth of his body feels unnaturally close to me, even through my coat. His presence is something physical, something distinct on my skin, and I find myself wondering how the night is going to end. I glance sideways at him, at his impressive figure in his expensive suit. And for a moment, I'm not exactly averse to the idea of not going home tonight.

The noise of the restaurant dims as we stroll along the concrete walkway, the bulk of the city rising behind us, and the massive expanse of the ocean glimmering enigmatically beyond the harbor. Many of the yachts moored here have lanterns in their rigging, and we pass one with a string of multi-colored lights, blue and red and green and yellow, bursting and swimming like bright beautiful fishes over the boat's white flanks, becoming murky and otherworldly in the harbor's dark waters.

Damien pauses and looks up at the lights. "How about we make some more skeletons?"

"What do you mean?"

The heat of his body abruptly leaves me as he drops my arm. He looks around him in an exaggerated, almost cartoonish fashion, and then he takes a quick hop onto the yacht's steps and climbs aboard.

"Damien!" I exclaim.

He presses his finger to his lips. "Shh! We're making skeletons, remember?" He holds out his hand to me.

I stare at him, then around at the deserted harbor, then back at him. He's not seriously thinking of taking his ghostwriter on a jaunt to steal a luxury yacht, is he? My eye catches sight of the name painted on the yacht's snowy flank: *Marlene*. The name rings a bell. And then I remember what he said in the restaurant.

Damien is still holding out his hand, and there's something almost pleading in his expression. I smile coyly. I take his hand and he swings me on board.

"Criminal," I reprimand.

"It's all for the book," he counters. He's still holding my hand. There's barely any space between us. I look up into his amazing eyes, feeling them burning into me. He raises his hand, brushes back a strand of my hair. My cheeks are tingling, like I've just drained half a bottle of whiskey, my heart thumping. Oh god, he's going to kiss me now. Is this a good idea? Do I want this?

But Damien's hand cups my cheek, lifts my chin, and I cease to think. He's already bending his head. I rise and kiss him, fierce and hungry.

For a second, he is still. And then he grabs me by the hips, crushing me against him. We're kissing and it's so hot and I can't think. Damien's hands are burning through my dress, and I twist my hand in his hair and he lifts me as though I weigh nothing at all. I wrap my legs around him, and he carries me down into the cabin.

*   *   *

Damien's fingers languidly trail down my back, tracing the channel of my spine. I look back over my shoulder at him. His hair is ruffled where I pulled it into disarray and his skin is flushed. When he looks up at me and meets my gaze, his eyes are so bright it's like looking into a naked flame.

"So, who's Marlene?"

There's a soft glow in his eyes. "Nobody."

"Come on, Damien. You named your boat after her."

"Nobody you need to be concerned about."

I turn my body towards him. "Okay, now I *absolutely* need to know."

He rolls his eyes, but he's smiling. "Just an old flame. She's the one that helped me discover all these feelings inside me. Untapped desires."

"Wow, must be quite a woman."

"Not as impressive as you." He chuckles. "This was another lifetime. I will tell you all about her someday."

We keep silent for a minute, looking at each other.

"What are you thinking?" I ask, bending my knee to touch him gently with my foot.

"About us." His fingers are warm and gentle. I smirk, closing my eyes, remembering what he could do with those supple digits. "About whether this will change our working relationship."

"Why should it?"

"Well. I have seduced you."

I laugh. "What makes you think I'm the seduced one?" I look over my shoulder at him.

He looks a little surprised, then thoughtful. "I suppose I didn't expect you to give in to me so easily."

My spine stiffens. I sit up, his hand falling away from me, and I cross my knees, reaching for the bedsheet to wrap around my shoulders.

"I don't mean that in a bad way," he says quickly. "Ah—fuck. Sorry. That came out all wrong."

"Yes, it did."

"I didn't mean to sound as though I were criticizing you for that." He reaches out and touches my exposed knee. "I promise." He smiles. "I enjoyed myself too much for that."

I look at his hand, then sigh. "Fine. You're forgiven."

"And you…?"

"Oh yes." My cheeks grow warm. "I had a really good time too."

"Good."

"And, well, I wanted to sleep with you. That's all. We're two consenting adults on equal footing. I can easily walk away from this, and so can you."

"Okay." He sounds a little disappointed.

"Did you want me to say I was driven wild with lust for you and no professional restraint could hold me back?" I tease.

He rolls his eyes. "Well, that wouldn't have been unpleasant to hear."

"I was mad with desire for you, Damien. I couldn't keep my hands off you."

He chuckles and shakes his head. "Don't."

"Don't worry, I'm a professional, you're safe now."

"A consummate professional?" He wiggles his eyebrows suggestively, and I burst out laughing.

"In a way, yes," I say, still grinning. "You'd be surprised how revealing pillow talk can be."

"So, this was all a setup then?" Damien strokes my knee, his fingers delightfully tickling my skin. "Just a ruse to worm my secrets out of me?" His hand is burning. His fingers creep higher, and I close my eyes.

"Yes," I whisper, my breath catching a little. "Anything for the biography."

"Anything," Damien whispers back, and my lips are already parted when he kisses me again.

*　　*　　*

I stay the night on the yacht, and the next morning Damien drops me off at my apartment. "I'll see you after the weekend?"

"Tuesday afternoon," I say.

"Great. I'll send a car."

"Okay." I reach for the door handle, but he grabs my wrist and kisses me hard, his lips pressing mine, then lets me go.

"Now you can go," he says, smiling from ear to ear.

Inside my flat, I go into the bathroom and stare at my face in the mirror. I splash cold water on my cheeks, touching my lips. I take a deep breath. I shower, brush my teeth, then meditate for a while, every sensation in my body coming to life and easing its way into my awareness. I sit with my thoughts for a long time, turning over the events of the past few days. Then I stretch, sit down at my desk, open my laptop, and get to work.

*　　*　　*

By the time Tuesday arrives, I've crafted what I'm going to say to Damien about that night in the yacht, despite how I felt about it then. *Boundaries are very important to me, Damien, especially in a complicated relationship like ours where the emphasis is on the professional.*

I do my hair repeatedly, unable to decide which style sends the most appropriate message. I hold my hair up in a ponytail and turn side to side in the mirror, watching the ends of my hair swish back and forth on my neck. Maybe I imagined the force in Damien's grip. Maybe I imagined how possessive his mouth was on mine.

I shake my head, letting my hair fall back down on my shoulders. I'm being ridiculous. It's not going to destroy my professional relationship with Damien to tell him I'd prefer a little warning next time. He can't take exception to that.

I let my hair stay down, brushed smooth and shiny. I keep my makeup simple. I choose a crisp white button-up shirt and black jeans—smart casual. Not to be taken advantage of, but not so intimidating that he won't listen. The thought that a prominent billionaire might be intimidated by a woman half his size is somewhat ludicrous, but I know how fragile male egos can be, especially the famous ones.

The car picks me up promptly at five o'clock and takes me to the harbor. I'd expected to meet with Damien at his office, and I'm annoyed that he didn't tell me we were going back to the yacht. His "stolen" yacht. I'm not quite sure what he wanted to achieve with that joke. Keep up the image of the dashing playboy, maybe, or make me think he was a criminal in order to…I don't know. Add spice to the biography? How much spice does he want?

It's already getting dark, and the harbor is deserted. Damien is waiting for me by the yacht, his brilliant eyes darkened and shadowed. "Hello, you," he says, kissing my cheek. Then he draws back, looking me in the face. "Are you okay?"

My anger thaws a little under his concern. "Yes. I thought we were meeting at the office."

"Ah, I thought the yacht would be more comfortable. We can have a couple of drinks, sit on a sofa instead of terrible office chairs."

"The chairs in your office probably cost more than I make

in a year."

"Well…" He laughs ruefully. "Is it wrong that I wanted to come here again?"

"No."

"Well…" He grins at me, then springs onboard the yacht in a mirror movement from the other night. "Come aboard the pirate ship, Hazel."

I roll my eyes, but his grin is infectious. "And you're the captain, I suppose."

"Certainly. Plundering the seas wherever I go, picking up fair maidens and treasure left, right, and center."

"Sexy." I take his hand and let him help me on board.

His grip on my wrist reminds me of my speech that I've prepared, and I'm about to mention the other day to him when he gives my arm a tug that pulls me forward, so I stumble against him.

He catches me, laughing. "Clumsy," he says, and brushes back a strand of my hair.

The obviousness of it is unbearably awkward. I manage half a laugh, avoiding his eyes. He still holds me close to him. Too close.

"Damien," I say, trying to match his light tone, and move my hand to signify that it's time for him to let go of my wrist.

He looks confused, then releases me. I titter, trying to cover up the moment, and say briskly—too loudly, I realize—"Well, shall we go and get that drink? I could murder a coffee."

Damien is still for a moment. I feel his gaze burning into the side of my face as I look away from him and toward the cabin. Then he says, "Sure. Yeah. That sounds great."

We head inside. I hadn't noticed much about the cabin last time we were in here, but it's beautiful, just like the outside of the yacht. Lots of jewel tones—azure curtains, a golden throw over the emerald sofa cushions, a dark ruby-red rug with turquoise and ochre embroidery. The cabin could easily look gauche, but somehow it gets away with it.

I sit down on the sofa, get out my laptop, and start my recorder. Damien goes to the sideboard. There is an array of alcohol bottles, but I'm glad to see him move past them and go to the espresso machine—a twin of the one inside his office. He takes out two white china mugs from the cupboard.

I take a deep breath. Now is when I should talk to him. But somehow, sitting here on his private yacht while he personally makes me coffee, my prepared speech sounds harsh. Ungrateful.

"Damien," I say.

He turns around, a steaming mug in each hand. "Black? I got in some oat milk if you wanted to take it white."

The thoughtfulness of that gesture takes me completely by surprise. "Uh, no, thank you," I stammer. "Black is fine. Thank you though."

"No problem."

He gives me my coffee, then sits down next to me on the sofa. I take a sip, even though it's too hot and burns my tongue.

"Right, then." Damien smiles and raises his mug in a toast to me. "How are you?"

"I'm…I'm good."

"Are you sure? You seem a little on edge."

"No, I…" I lift one shoulder. "Just thinking about how we're going to navigate all this."

"All this?"

"You. Me. The book."

"The book." He sighs. "You make it sound like the other woman."

"It is, in a way. The book should be our priority."

"Not having amazing sex on a beautiful private yacht?"

"Exactly."

Damien looks into his coffee. He sighs again. "I was worried about this."

"Not worried enough to not sleep with me," I point out, his tone irritating me a little.

"Last time you basically admitted that *you* seduced *me*."

"I think it was a joint effort, Damien."

He shrugs. "Okay."

"I don't regret it," I say. "I had a really nice time, and the meal was amazing and— But you can't act like you're the wounded party and like you were worried about this all along."

"All I meant was, I'm aware that situations like this can get complicated. I wasn't worried about you, per se. I know you're a professional. *You* can handle this." He looks out of the yacht's dark window. "It depends on who's involved. It can get confusing for them."

I'm not sure what he's talking about. I stare at him, but he carries on looking away from me. He reminds me of nothing as much as a character in a film having a flashback to their tragic backstory. Is that the image he's trying to create? It's never occurred to me before just how skilled he must be at creating the impression he wants. He's had years of working with photographers and creative directors. He must have had so much experience at setting a scene, creating an ambience, telling a story in his actions and gestures and poses.

He finally brings his gaze back from the window. "You're

different," he says.

"Different to whom?"

He shakes his head. "It doesn't matter."

My anger rises. I can tell when I'm being manipulated. I've had years of being underestimated in my chosen profession, and years of men expecting to know what I'm thinking and feeling. My voice comes out razor-sharp. "Don't play with me, Damien. Is this a skeleton you want me to ask about, or a skeleton you want to keep to yourself?"

"I don't know what you're talking about."

"Then why are you talking about it?"

We stare at each other.

Then Damien smiles. "Oh, I'm sorry." He puts the coffee down. "I am being coy. I suppose I just want to make sure I don't repeat mistakes."

"What kind of mistakes?"

"Oh, nothing really." He grins at me, that easy charm flashing up warm and bright. "But I'm sure you've dealt with young people before. Interns and assistants who get the wrong idea. You know. They act one way and then another and then cry about it to anyone who'll listen."

My brain is struggling to understand exactly what he's talking about—what he might be talking about, he hasn't said anything definite yet…

"Young women can be fragile," I say carefully.

"Yes, exactly." His voice is light. He doesn't even notice that I said women instead of people. "You know how it is."

"They have an idea of how you're going to be and act and it's a shock to them when you're a real human like them."

"Yes." He leans back and crosses his legs, beaming. "You see. I wasn't worried at all about you, Hazel. You're special."

My hands are freezing cold, but I push back my hair and smile at him. "Well, I did ace my interview after all."

He laughs, loud and confident. "Yes, you did." He reaches out his arm and places it around my shoulders. The heat of his body burns through our clothes, spreading through me, and I close my eyes, thinking of the last time we were here on this yacht. It seems a very long time ago now.

"Hey." Damien smiles down at me. "You okay?"

"Yes." I make myself smile back at him. "Yes, I'm fine."

"Are you sure? You look a little spooked. I haven't said anything that might upset you, have I?"

"No, no, really I'm fine."

Frustration—disappointment?—flashes across his face before vanishing under his smooth smile. "Good. That's good."

We sit in silence for a moment, until he removes his arm and says, "Well, I suppose we should get some work done."

"*Don't worry, I've been taking notes.*" The words leave my mouth before I think about their consequences.

Damien's body freezes. He's so close to me that I can feel every muscle in his body tighten. "You've been recording all of this?"

His voice is strange. Low. Tight. Thrumming with a kind of excitement.

"Not to worry," I say, and my voice is too high, too quick. Don't make him angry—de-escalate this, it'll be okay. "I can delete the file. It's okay."

"Why would I want you to delete the file? I've not said anything incriminating. Or wrong. Have I, Hazel?"

I try to laugh. To think of something to say that will smooth this over, but all my words have vanished.

Damien makes a movement, and I startle to my feet, stumbling away from the sofa, away from him. My laptop and recorder are on top of my bag, on top of the table. Damien's fingers close around the recorder. He brings it to his face and examines it as though he's never seen anything like it before. He pushes one of the buttons and my own panicked voice shrills out: "Don't worry, I've been taking notes."

I take another step back towards the stairs as Damien gets to his feet. "I'll delete it," I gabble. "I swear, I'll delete it, you can trash the recorder, you can burn it or break it or—"

"How do I know you haven't transferred the file somewhere else?" Damien's voice is soft. His eyes are blazing strange, unnatural blue fire. "Set up an auto-sync. Or a stream of some kind. The Internet is forever, isn't it?" He prowls forward.

"I haven't, Damien, that would be a total breach of trust, I wouldn't—"

"Trust?" He laughs. He sounds so excited. "How can you talk to me about trust? Is that what all this has been about? Getting the job, seducing me, coming to the yacht, all so you can publish a dirty little story about a man—a *good* man, mind you, Hazel—who hasn't done anything wrong? So you can spread lies about me? Like they *tried* to?"

"Damien—"

"And to record it all—openly! To my face!"

I bump into the sideboard, jostling the drink bottles. The sound distracts me, and in that second, Damien has me. Gripping both my arms, he pins me against the wall. Right away I detect a few things that I had inexplicably missed before. Alcohol in his breath. Slightly red-rimmed eyes. "What are you not telling me?" His voice is raspy.

My heart is hammering in my chest. "Don't know what you mean. I'm not hiding anything from you. Honest to god!"

He stands there holding me for a moment longer, before letting go of my arms.

He takes a step back and stammers, "Sorry Hazel, don't know what came over me."

I rub the side of my arms where he gripped me. "I should go." Staggering past him, I go to the table and start collecting my things.

Damien runs his fingers through his silver hair. "It was a mistake. Give me another chance." Instead of responding, I sling my handbag on my shoulder and amble towards the stairs. I look back, making sure that he isn't following me.

"I said I was sorry," he persists, eyes pleading.

I climb two at a time, keeping my face straight.

"See you Friday in the office?" he bellows as I swing the door open and burst into the cool night air.

*   *   *

I toss and turn in my bed. I can feel the silky smoothness of the Egyptian cotton sheet under me, caressing my bare skin. The temperature of the room is just right, my body is snug and warm under the fluffy duvet. And yet, the elusive slumber keeps evading me.

The event from earlier occupies my mind. This gig is

significant. And fascinating. Just like he is. Can't remember the last time anything brought up so much excitement in me. But the sudden change in him was terrifying.

He's definitely hiding something from me. Does he think I know what it is? I've been recapping our encounters from the beginning, hoping to glimpse a clue or two.

If I must guess, it's possibly something to do with the women he dated. Those *heartbreakers*. Damien certainly doesn't seem like the type to forgive and forget so easily. Did he make them pay? It'd be great if I could get some face time with his ex-lovers. I bet they have some interesting things to say about him.

Marlene.

It is strange how he would bring up a certain topic only to quickly dismiss it when I start to probe more. I'm beginning to question the validity of some of his stories. Like the mention of young women under him who got the wrong idea. I smell lawsuits from miles away. Have to dig more.

With a sigh I sit up, tossing my sleep mask aside. There's no sleeping for this girl now. I turn on the light from the side table and pick up a book. Then something alerts me. Was it a sound? Could be anything really. I shift my attention back to the book, opening the bookmarked pages.

There it is again. A dull thud. I close the book and put it away. I get up and slip on a bathrobe. It's probably nothing, but I'm curious.

I open the bedroom door and step outside. Everything seems normal at first glance. Nearing the study, I notice a faint pool of obscured light seeping from under the door. The blinds must have been left open. Unhurriedly but anxiously, I reach for the handle. It is cold to the touch. Damn window must be open too. The door has been left slightly ajar. I push. The groans of the hinges make me cringe.

It's a complete mess. Filing drawers are flung open. Papers and folders are strewn about on the carpet and on the desk. A picture frame is knocked facedown. A glass is lying on its side, spilling the brown contents onto the loose stack of papers.

I'm about to turn around when a silhouette stirs.

With unexpected agility and force, it pulls me into the room. I find myself in a chokehold facing the window. The attacker is perked up behind me. I try to pull the arm encircling my neck. But it gets even tighter. I feel a familiar heat from his touch, the sensation that had lingered on my skin, not too long ago. There's a sudden heaviness in my chest.

"Where's the safe?" The voice is hoarse, like sandpaper grinding.

"Huh? Wh...what safe?" I stutter.

"Where you put the valuable stuff."

"Don't have one..."

"Are you lying to me?" His arm stiffens.

Gasping for air, I clutch and pull. "No, I swear!" My vision blurs. Desperate, I stretch my arm back. With clawed fingers, I grab and squash. A shriek. I'm suddenly free. Hungrily I devour air. My hand rubbing my neck. Then I quickly turn around.

A man is pressing his thighs together. Hands groping his crotch. "You, bitch!" He bares his fangs. He's dressed in black. Head to toe. A balaclava conceals his identity. But his real voice and physique give him away. My body goes cold with dread. My suspicion is justified.

With both hands still massaging my tender neck, I glare at him with an open mouth. "You! Why?"

Damien grimaces. "Hand over all the materials. I want them destroyed."

"Wha…what? There's nothing there." A feeling of hopelessness creeps up from the pit of my stomach.

"Quit playing dumb. I know what you're up to!"

I gulp hard. "Whatever you suspect, it's all in your head. You're delusional. And paranoid!"

He scowls and begins to plod closer. I take two steps back.

"You want it? Fine. Take everything! Burn it, see if I care!" My hands are trembling, suspended in front of my body as if deflecting invisible incoming missiles.

He advances forward. Just a few feet away now. I keep retreating. Stopped by the wall.

I gasp. "Please. Think for a sec! What are you gonna do with me?"

With a jerk, he takes off his mask. "Hand it over and I'm gone."

"I'm at your mercy. I've got nothing. It's the truth!" I bawl. Spittle sprays from my lips.

"That's what they all say." He lunges forward. I swing my arm. My clenched fist connects with his ear. He grumbles. Then he comes at me again. Grabs my arm with force. Twists it up behind me. Something cracks.

White agony shoots from my shoulder down to every fingertip. I scream. I flail. I scratch and kick. He shrieks.

Then he seizes me by the throat, smashing me back against him. His body heat sears through me.

"Hazel," he whispers. Just like when he was on top of me. Hands on my hips. Spending himself deep inside me.

He inhales. I realize he's smelling my hair.

I try to speak, but no words come out. There's no air. The world is closing in.

He grunts. I taste copper. He presses my body against his. His fingers breaking my skin. A crushing sound.

My vision turns red. Then black. Then nothing at all.

*　　*　　*

My fingers drum on the desk, right foot tapping the floor, with no particular set rhythm.

I check my reflection in the dark screen of my dead laptop. My face is blurred. Indistinct.

I take some deep breaths, just as I was taught at that company-mandated wellness seminar. Probably the only thing I got out of that funeral dirge. That and a steak lunch.

"Damien?" Stephanie pokes her head in the office door. "Are you ready for her?"

I nod. "Send her in."

Stephanie vanishes. I look at my fingers, trying to make them be still in my lap. I rub my thighs in anticipation.

After a few moments, Stephanie knocks on my door and ushers in my two o'clock.

I didn't send out a public call for interviewees like last time. I made a few calls, asked around, kept things discreet. Deborah's name came up in a conversation, and after putting out a few feelers I knew I had to have her. She's young—younger than I expected— but already gathering an impressive array of bylines and contacts.

She extends her hand to me before I've even gotten up from

my chair. "Mr. Wolfenstein," she says, "pleased to meet you."

Her hand grips mine. Her eyes flash emerald-green, and her hair is ebony-dark, cut into a sleek bob. Suddenly I have this overwhelming urge to run my hands through it.

"Please," I say, smiling. "Call me Damien."

I expect a slight flush, maybe a demure look down. But neither happens. Her inquisitive eyes bore deep into me. She holds onto my hand for a second longer than anticipated.

"Damien," she says. Her voice is brisk. "Thank you for arranging this meeting."

"Not at all. Thank you for meeting me. I'm sure you're very busy."

"I am," she says, without a flicker of humility. "But the project sounded very interesting." She grins, showing perfect white pearly teeth. Her lips are full, painted a dark berry color.

"Great fangs! Did you have braces?" I interpose, attempting to throw her off.

"All-natural, fortunate enough to be born with these." She smirks.

I can't tell what's stronger, my annoyance at her arrogance or my arousal at her appearance.

"Well, I'm glad you're intrigued enough to be here," I utter with a self-deprecating chuckle. "And even if the subject matter is poor, you're skilled enough to make it interesting. I particularly enjoyed your article on Senator Kelly. The way you held his feet to the fire over the union kickbacks. That took some balls."

"Thank you." She nods but doesn't seem flattered by the compliment. Not even a smile. "I heard you had a writer?"

"Yes. She's missing. There was a suspected break-in. Poor

soul. But even before that, we…" I can't think of a good phrase to describe how my relationship with Hazel degenerated. How she completely betrayed me and lost my trust. "We had different visions for the end result," I say.

"What vision did they have?"

I look at her closely. Eyes narrowed. Lips pursed. At least Hazel was affable. Deborah sits with her hands folded in her lap, one knee crossed over the other. Confident. Beautiful. Talented. Curious.

"It doesn't matter," I say. "Does it?"

"It's helpful to know that kind of thing," she says. "So I don't repeat the same mistakes."

I can hear there's something else in her voice now. Something veiled. She knows something.

I shrug, making it look casual, as though the matter isn't at all important. "She just didn't understand the direction I wanted to go in. The tone, the feel, all of that."

"I see."

Does she? Does she see? What does she see?

She cracks a smile. Just like Hazel, and the others, she intends to use me. She wants to dig up all my past and parade it out for the world to see. She wants to see me toppled from grace. From power. Laughed at. Everything about me forgotten except my mistakes and the lies flogged to sell papers.

"So, what direction do *you* want to go in?" she asks. Deborah. So clever. So talented.

"I have a definite idea," I say. "Came up with a list of things I'd like to go over with you."

"That sounds great."

Of course it does. She's wet just thinking about the seduction, the reveal, the scoop, the book deal, the talk-show interviews.

"Let's table the brainstorming for now." More of an order than a suggestion. "The office is so stifling for creativity. Prefer a more comfortable environment."

"That's totally fine," she says, flashing those tremendous teeth again. "Wherever you'll feel most at ease."

"There's a restaurant at the harbor that does amazing steak. Unless you're vegetarian?"

"No, not at all."

"Excellent. How does a working dinner sound?"

"It would be a pleasure, thank you."

"Excellent. Excellent." I beam at her. The heat is building inside me.

Like before. Many tried. And failed. Deborah will soon be just another memento.

I'm Damien Wolfenstein. My skeletons are staying buried.

NO PLACE LIKE HOME

"Last one downstairs is doing the dishes tonight!" chirps Cyndi. She and her younger brother, Trevor, are racing down the stairs. They giggle and jostle as each tries to get ahead of the other. Cyndi wins the race quite convincingly. "Hah! I win! I win!" She does a celebratory jig.

"Not fair! You were two steps ahead from the start!" whines Trev.

"A little bird told me we're having icky sticky cinnamon buns for dessert." She ignores his plea. "Have fun with the dishes!" Trev blows a raspberry.

"Play nice, Cyndi!" a warm, feminine voice emanates from the kitchen.

"Yeah, Cyndi!" Trev chimes in with a grin.

"Okay, guess I'll help with dishes," Cyndi raises her shoulders and jokingly pouts. "Mama's boy!" She mumbles the words while covering her mouth with her hands and pretending to cough. Trev makes a face.

They both grin at the smell of their mother's breakfast wafting through the air. Pancakes, their favorite.

"Did you sign Trev's report card, dear?" Rebecca asks her

husband as she plops a pile of microwaved hotcakes in front of her son.

"Yes, dear," Jordan smiles as he tightens his necktie, then leans over and kisses his wife on the cheek. "Nice earrings, Bec," he exclaims, knowing that they are the ones he gave her for their last anniversary.

"You know they're my favorite," Rebecca beams as she sets a plate in front of her daughter, then unconsciously touches the diamond teardrop dangle of her gold earrings.

Jordan stands still, eyes filled with awe. His wife has a delicate nose, high cheekbones, and lustrous auburn hair. Her hazel eyes are captivating. She used to model and act but gave it all up with the first pregnancy.

As Jordan puts on his suit coat, he winks and flashes her a smile. It's so bewitching that it would fill a rotting, dying soul with joy.

Rebecca slips between her children and holds up her phone. "Selfie time!" she announces as the kids look up and crack a smile. A few loud clicking sounds. Rebecca then gives them each a peck on the cheek.

"Instagram post number three hundred and thirty-eight," she mumbles as she returns to her phone.

"You guys won't believe this," she shrieks. "We got over sixty-two thousand likes for our Caribbean holiday pics! New Moore post record!" Her eyes twinkle as the Moores squeal and high-five each other.

"Thanks to my boyish charm and these deadly dimples," Trevor exclaims, twitching his eyebrows.

"Gross!" Cyndi disagrees. "Got to be my beautiful picture

among the flamingos."

Jordan smirks. "Talk all you want. We wouldn't get past a hundred likes if it weren't for my good-looking mug and six-pack abs in a swimming trunk!"

Everyone roars at that.

"Okay, kids. Since I'm the only MATURE adult in this household, I command thee to finish your breakfast and get ready." Rebecca speaks in an authoritative voice but miserably fails at suppressing laughter.

The kids each shove another mouthful of pancake into their mouths. They giggle as Jordan attempts to imitate his wife with a duck voice.

Jordan Moore is a software developer, a rather contemporary job for a man his age, but he has always been one to keep up with the times. Even at forty-two, he doesn't look a day over thirty-five. His jet-black hair, tan skin, and handsome, chiseled face captured Rebecca's heart. Still do.

Rebecca Moore, on the other hand, proclaims to be a SAHM, but she runs a very successful vlog, "Moore Fun with Rebecca," where she shares her family dynamics and children's joyful antics to her quarter of a million subscribers. In her free time, she shows houses for fun.

"Alright, kiddos," Rebecca prattles as she grabs her briefcase and scoots across the floor in her four-inch stilettos, "Dad's taking you to school this morning, and you are walking home this afternoon." Looking at Trevor, she says, "Don't forget to hand in your report card. I'm sure Marvin remembers this, but please remind him to bring his swimming trunks next week. 'Cause I'm taking you guys to the new waterpark. Woohoo!" Then she glances towards Cyndi. "Eat your veggies! Make sure you have your brother and the two of you come straight home. If I'm not here yet, I will only be several minutes behind you…lock the door. Kiss, kiss." She blows air kisses their way and flies out the door.

The children gaze at the door, smiling from ear to ear. Then they look at their dad.

Jordan shakes his head. "Oof, she's too much at times, isn't she? Wait till she gets to plan you guys' weddings!" The kids titter at this.

"Don't tell Mom I said that!" Jordan whispers as he tickles them and collects their plates.

As Jordan rushes his family out the door and towards the car, he swiftly puts the morning dishes in the washer. Then he heads out too, switching the security system on and locking the door behind him.

Before pulling out of the driveway to head towards the school, he takes out his phone to do what he does every morning. He texts his wife the message he had sent her after they became a couple, a tradition he has kept going for fifteen years now.

I'm so lucky to have you in my life. And I'm counting the stars until I can behold your face once again. Love Jordan, your one and only…and the kids.

He likes to imagine her smiling face each time she receives the text.

* * *

Jordan pulls into the driveway. It was a tough day at work with a rather substantial fire he had to put out, so to speak. A major client decided to move up their deadline and threatened to leave when given a no for an answer. With a little bit of luck, he masterfully negotiated a new, workable deadline with the client. And, just as essential, he managed to get reinforcements from his boss, in the form of extra bodies and approved OTs. Frankly, the thought of coming home to his wife and kids was just the thing that got him through the day.

Breathing a sigh of relief, he opens the car door and gets out.

It's apparent from outside the house that his family is home. The sound of the television playing, the raucous laughter of his kids, and the smell of Rebecca's cooking excite him. He swings the door open to the alarm sounding.

Quickly he slams in the code on the worn buttons and sets his briefcase down.

His head cocks to the side when he realizes that his wife's case isn't there. Strange, considering they both always put theirs next to each other so they can easily be found the next day.

"Daddy," Cyndi runs up to her dad and wraps her arms around his neck.

She stands on her tiptoes to reach, but she manages.

"Pops," Trevor says, as he fist bumps his father.

"Hey, princess," Jordan says, as he kisses his daughter on the head, while closing in on the bump, but something catches him off guard.

The slight glimpse of a blonde-headed woman in the kitchen catches his attention. He can only see her backside, but he knows it isn't Rebecca.

"Who's in the kitchen with your mother?" Jordan asks, eyebrows raised.

"Oh, Mom's not here," Trevor casually states as he goes back to the Nintendo Switch in his hand.

He walks back into the living room without blinking an eye, leaving Cynthia and her father in the small entry room.

"What does he mean, 'Mom's not home,' Cyndi?" Jordan queries, sounding a tad concerned.

He tries to rein in his worry, for his daughter's sake. His wife was always there, but that wasn't the part that confuses him. If his wife is gone, then who's the blonde in the kitchen?

"Oh, that's Mandy," Cyndi announces, looking back towards the kitchen. "We came home to her fixing dinner in there."

Without saying another word, Jordan slides past his daughter and heads towards the kitchen.

"Excuse me," he says. "Who are you? Where's Rebecca?"

"Oh," the woman turns around and wipes her hands on the towel over her shoulder. She's in her mid- to late-thirties, with long, dirty blonde hair tied up in a bun. She has a Grecian nose, sharp eyes, and full lips. Her makeup is a little overdone, but it fails to hide a small, hairline scar that sits just under her left temple. And upon closer inspection, there's an even tinier one on her chin.

"Sorry, didn't mean to startle you. The name is Mandy." She reaches out to shake his hand, but he's more than reluctant. "Your wife's friend…she had an emergency with a client and asked me to be here when the kids and you got home. I told her I would fix dinner for the three of you. She said she may be late."

"I've never heard of you. How'd you get into the house?" Jordan is scratching his temple.

"We met a few days ago at Old Town Grocery and we just clicked. She has a boy and a girl. I had, have a boy and a girl. Similar ages too, would you believe that? But like I said, Rebecca had something urgent she needed to attend to and begged me to tend to the family while she's away. She gave me her keys and the passcode to the security system. Nine, two, four, three, one," she spouts off.

Jordan is more than suspicious, even though the woman is right…that is the code to their security system, and his wife's keys were lying on the counter, but if he didn't know better, her car key was on the chain too. How is she gone in her car if the keys are there, he wonders.

"Okay, well, what's so urgent that she would just leave her family? Not even a text?" Jordan checks his phone again.

"She wouldn't say exactly," the woman named Mandy answers. "Just something about a client…it sounded serious, to be honest."

Jordan ignores what the woman is saying and dials his wife on speed dial.

You've got Becca, leave your name and number at the beep, if this is Jordan, Trevor, or Cyndi, I love you.

Then the beep sounds.

"Honey, please call me back as soon as you can, your friend…" he hesitates to say that word, "Well, she says you are busy with a client, but you are always home at this time." He pauses. "Just call me back please, I love you."

He then hangs up and calls back again, then he sends a text.

911, call home asap!

"There's no reason to be alarmed, I'm sure she will call back soon," Mandy says with a wide smile on her face.

"I just don't get it," Jordan says.

"Get what?" Mandy asks.

"Why would she ask you instead of her best friend who lives

just a couple of blocks away?"

"Maybe the friend wasn't available. I don't know," Mandy prattles, her voice getting louder and squeakier as she goes.

Jordan returns to his phone. He presses the buttons and brings the phone to his ear. While the phone is dialing, Jordan watches Mandy with slightly squinted eyes. Her face is without expression. "Hello Stace, Jordan here. Sorry to bother. Have you seen Becs?" A pause. "Is that right? Okay, thanks. Yeah, been calling her. I'm sure she's just distracted with something, somewhere. You know how she is sometimes." A dry chuckle. "Will do, thanks again!" He hangs up and tries Rebecca's parents as well. No luck.

"I was just trying to help out a friend. I'm sure she'll be back soon." Mandy then leans closer and whispers into Jordan's ear, making his hair stand on end. "Let's not worry the children, shall we? I promise, it will all be alright."

"Well, thank you," Jordan pulls away. "I can take care of the kids from here. Thanks for fixing supper for us." He motions her towards the door, but she doesn't budge.

"Why don't we eat dinner," Mandy chirps, ignoring Jordan's worry. "I made mac and cheese," she announces to the children in the next room.

The children's cheers flow from the other room.

Jordan is on high alert, but the kids seem to be fond of Mandy. He doesn't understand that part at all. He and Rebecca had taught their children not to talk to strangers, and Mandy is as strange as they come, in his book. He's trying very hard to remember if he's met her before. Or if Rebecca ever told him about Mandy.

He steps back and watches her, the woman whom he can't find it in his heart to trust, loading the table with food that he doesn't want to eat. But above all, he doesn't want to worry his children, so he will likely partake in the meal.

As he sits down at the table, he flips open his phone one more time and looks for missed calls, anything, and then he notices it. He just realizes that she hadn't replied to his text from this morning, like she always does.

*   *   *

During dinner, Jordan tries to act normal in front of the kids. It's the hardest thing he has ever done. So many unanswered questions eat at him as he feels it deep down inside, that something is amiss.

He watches Mandy like a hawk and to him, it seems like she's done this hundreds of times before, as part of a family…maybe even as part of *this* family.

The way she knows her way around the kitchen is a flashing red flag to Jordan. Even if she were Rebecca's friend, and Rebecca had shown Mandy the kitchen, Jordan knows there is no way this woman would know where everything is. She finds things with unsettling ease.

To him, it's like Mandy had been in his home before. Hundreds of times, perhaps. And yet, he doesn't know squat about her.

Even the way she's interacting with the kids feels unnatural. Jordan is hating himself for letting them act like a normal family at the dinner table, but his kids are devouring their food and seem fine. So, to keep up with appearances, he drinks and eats. Besides, he needs more information from Mandy, but he has to tread carefully.

"Looks to me you know the house really well. Are you here often?"

Mandy nods. "Uh-huh. A few times."

"Becs must have given you quite a thorough tour of the house. You even know where we store tea bags."

"Yeah, she's an exceptional realtor for sure," Mandy replies, "And I have an excellent memory."

"Good for you," Jordan comments drily. "Where did you two meet again? Old Town on Beecher?"

"No, silly. There's no grocery store on Beecher, you know that!" Mandy sneers. "It's on Bay Road. A block away from the church."

After dinner, the kids insist that they go to the living room, back to the TV. Jordan hadn't even thought about the Nintendo Switch Trevor had in his hands when he got home. Trevor doesn't have a Nintendo Switch, or any game system at that. Rebecca and Jordan wanted to keep their kids from rotting their young brains out.

His suspicion fueled even more, Jordan jets to the living room, still looking as casual as he can, so as not to alarm the kids. Open boxes are strewn about the room, something else he hadn't noticed. He was more concerned about the woman in the kitchen than the things that weren't normally there.

"What's all this?" Jordan asks his kids, kneeling and sifting through the packages. The colorful, thick boxes and the fancy wrappings look expensive. These are definitely not the dollar-store varieties.

"Mandy brought us these," Cyndi says, as she paints her nails with her new polish…something else Jordan and Rebecca don't allow. They wanted to give their daughter makeup and nail polish for her thirteenth birthday, as a sort of rite of passage.

They take turns showing off their loot. The latest iPad, hoverboard, among others. Jordan and Rebecca would frown upon most of it. They believe that if the children have everything in their early years, they won't appreciate anything in the future. Makeup and game console at thirteen, a car for practicing driving at fifteen, savings accounts at sixteen, work with Dad at eighteen, college funds, it's all in their plan…or was, Jordan thinks to himself.

"This is too much," Jordan says as he turns to storm back into the kitchen, but Mandy is there waiting behind him. That startles him.

"Why would you give us presents? Particularly ones that I KNOW Rebecca would have never approved."

"Oh, it's nothing, I asked your wife first. In fact, some of these were her suggestions," Mandy states matter-of-factly.

"That's impossible," Jordan denies, trying not to lift his voice. "These are all things that Becs and I have decided to milestone into OUR children's lives."

"She didn't tell me that." Mandy lifts her chin. "I've only known Rebecca for a few days and yet I trust and love her like a sister already. She's helped me so much. Keeps talking about you guys and I feel like you're my own." Mandy shakes her head. "It's silly, isn't it? To want to gift people that I barely know. Only because I already love them through Rebecca."

Jordan doesn't answer as he clenches his fists.

"Can we keep our gifts, Daddy?" Trevor asks his father but doesn't get an answer back. Jordan keeps his eyes fixed on Mandy, fuming inwardly.

"Oh, not to worry, big boy, I got something for you, too,"

Mandy chatters, picking up a box off the couch and handing it to Jordan.

"I don't know about this," he hesitates as he hands the box back to Mandy, but she doesn't take it. "I'm not comfortable receiving this."

"Oh silly," Mandy dismisses him, hand gesturing for Jordan to open the box.

"Yeah, Dad," Trevor chimes in.

"We want to see what you got," Cyndi adds.

"It's not even Christmas, your birthday, or anniversary." Trevor is grinning from ear to ear. "It's not every day you get gifts to open."

Jordan looks at his son and smiles. In order not to alarm the children of his concerns, he opens the box while looking Mandy in the eye. He drops the box to the ground, taking out an expensive-looking tie.

"You like it?" Mandy looks at him with wide, expectant eyes.

Jordan is at a loss. Despite his protest, Mandy advances to put the tie on him. He attempts to take it out of her hand, but she pushes forward and wraps her arms around his shoulders to place the tie where it belongs.

"You look sharp," Mandy says. "You didn't have that color in your collection."

Jordan cocks his head to the side and stares at her blankly. He is utterly bewildered.

"How do you know that?" he asks her, voice quavering. This is way too personal for his liking. Jordan glares as Mandy stammers for a moment before replying.

"I asked your wife for a suggestion," Mandy offers. "She

knew I was gifting you three, and that was the only thing she could think of for you…said that's what she gets you every year for your anniversary."

"These things are private matters which my wife would have never told you. Not even her best friend knows our tie tradition. What's going on here?"

Mandy reaches up and puts her hand on his chest to calm him down. Jordan instinctively grabs her arm and twists her wrist. Mandy shrieks as Jordan notices the palpable tension in the room. The kids are staring at him with fear in their eyes.

He has never scared his kids before…he's never physical, not even when Trevor accidentally spilled Coke on his annual budget report. In his mind, this feels more like protection than anything. But of course, they don't see it that way.

He lets go of her wrist quickly, then backs up a little.

"You're scaring them!" Mandy blusters as she hugs Cyndi to her chest and pulls Trevor in for a hug. They don't resist. That hurts him.

After clearing his throat, he declares, "We need to talk in private."

"I'm just trying to be a friendly neighbor and you are treating me like some criminal!" Mandy rants.

Jordan rubs his eyes and massages his temple for a moment, collecting his thoughts. "Now you're a neighbor?" he asks with gritted teeth.

"Come on, kids, let's get ready for bed." She pulls them along with her. "Don't worry about Dad, he's just tired and confused," she finishes, steering the kids towards the stairs.

Jordan sighs as he picks up his phone and tries calling Rebecca once again.

You've got Becca, leave your name and number at the beep.

Jordan hangs up and tosses his phone down onto the side table. He flops down on the couch and buries his face in his hands.

* * *

Jordan is sitting at the edge of the chair by the door. He's itching to just take off and look for his wife but refuses to leave his kids with *her*.

He stands up and gazes in the mirror that sits over the entry table. Jordan looks at the tie tied around his neck with contempt. His wife would have never chosen it, Rebecca doesn't like salmon on him.

He jerks and pulls the tie off his neck and slams it down on the floor. He sits back down and picks his phone up. A noise catches his attention, and he looks towards the steps leading to the second floor of the house.

Mandy sashays down the stairs, alone. As he watches her descend the steps, there are a few things he realizes quickly: her face is rid of all the makeup that had been there before, her hair is wet and let loose, and she's wearing one of Rebecca's bathrobes.

"Don't make too much noise, they're finally asleep," Mandy says as she hits the ground floor barefoot. Without makeup, her scars are very visible, yet they don't blemish her innocent, pleasant look.

"They were restless. You upset them, what's wrong with you?" Mandy asks as she gives him a *you-naughty-boy* look.

Jordan shoots up out of the chair and strides towards her.

"I need some answers," Jordan demands. His jaw clenches.

"No more bullshit answers."

"I can't tell you what I don't know," Mandy responds sweetly. "Like I said, she was desperate and didn't offer an explanation, just called and begged for my assistance. Came running and here I am." She finishes that part with a smirk. "End of story."

"I know you're hiding something from me," Jordan says with an air of resoluteness. "What is it?"

"Maybe she's planning a surprise for you, Mr. Grumpypants. Or maybe she's owed some people money and had to figure a way to return it?"

"That's not possible," Jordan retorts.

"You think you know someone, but everyone has a secret they keep. Especially from those they love," Mandy chuckles.

"What are you saying?" Jordan demands. "I have no secrets I keep from my wife…"

"Maybe she just got tired of this perfect life, and she craved an adventure, some excitement," Mandy teases and then gets super close to Jordan. "Or maybe you manhandled her like you just did me, and she wanted to teach you a lesson?"

"You're talking out of your ass," Jordan asserts, his voice growing louder. "You don't know her…you don't know me…I have never touched my wife in anger a day in my life! Now, where is she?"

"Obviously, you don't know her, either. Not really. For all we know, she could be running away with a mysterious stranger for good! That diabolical cunt!" Mandy sneers. "Whatever—"

Jordan slaps Mandy across the face hard. He had never hit a woman before. Hell, he had never struck anyone in his whole life.

"Don't you ever fucking talk about her that way! Rebecca is

my wife, and we love each other!" Jordan proclaims.

Mandy stands stunned. Her mouth is twitching.

"I don't understand. Why are you treating me like this? What have I done that is so bad?" Mandy queries innocently. Her left cheek has started to redden. "You're supposed to be my knight in shining armor!"

Jordan feels insuppressible rage build up inside his chest. He pushes her against the wall across from them and grabs her neck. Mandy is choking and tearing up as he squeezes harder with his hands.

"I'm not your anything!" Jordan hisses through his teeth. "For the last time, where…is…my…wife?"

Without blinking, Mandy suddenly gives Jordan an uppercut. It doesn't really connect with Jordan's chin, but it is disruptive enough to make him falter. The grip on Mandy's neck loosens for a split second, enough to allow her to abruptly throw herself to one side. In the rush, the bathrobe comes undone just enough for Jordan to realize she's wearing Rebecca's sexy black lingerie underneath.

"What the—" Jordan begins, but he is cut short when he realizes how much Mandy looks like a lunatic: her neck is pink, hair unkempt and eyes bulging out. She looks like a bull seeing red as she stammers for words.

"I wanted to play nice, but you just have to ruin everything! Can't you just play along? Is that too much to ask?" Mandy mutters, her breath coming in waves.

"Is this what it's all about? Playing house?" Jordan scoffs, his upper lip curls. "Seducing me? Not a chance in hell! You're a fucking creep!"

Instead of lashing out, Mandy cracks a smile and crosses her arms across her chest.

"So where do you think she is then?" She is way too calm.

Jordan bunches his fists. "You tell me!"

"Humor me, take a guess," Mandy tosses her hair aside, as Jordan stares at her blankly. "Do you reckon it's just a coincidence that on the day your wife disappears, a stranger shows up in your home? Me, the creep," she purrs with venom in her voice.

"So, you know where she is?" Jordan holds his breath.

"Maybe."

"Did you kidnap her?"

Mandy snickers, "That is such an ugly word, don't you think? I'm borrowing a chapter in her life is all."

"You bitch!" Jordan raises his voice. "What did you do with her? That's my wife…the mother of my children."

"The question you should be asking is what could I do to her next?" Mandy teases, causing Jordan to freeze. "And the answer really depends on you."

"How so?" Jordan asks, despite knowing the answer to the question.

"You figure it out, Sherlock. All this racket is making me tired," Mandy says as she fake-yawns and stretches. "I think I'm gonna lie down on her bed."

"No, I need answers. I wanna talk to her," Jordan pleads as Mandy starts heading to the stairs, brushing past him.

Jordan puts a hand to her shoulder. Mandy turns her head sharply, giving him a piercing laser glare.

"I'd be very, very careful of what I say and do, if I were you. I may or may not know where your wife is, and," she looks up the steps, "those little angels have an awful habit of trusting strangers a little too easily. It would be no challenge at all to have them…" she pauses for effect, "whisked away." Mandy finishes and leers as Jordan lets go of her, mouth agape.

She climbs up the stairs very deliberately. Then, at the top landing, she casually glances down and says, "Oh, and thanks for taking the couch. If I were you, I wouldn't think about going anywhere, either." She sneers, sauntering down the hall.

Jordan desperately tries Rebecca's number a couple more times, to no avail. He has never felt so lost and helpless. All he can do is anxiously pace the room.

*　*　*

The next morning, Mandy returns to her cheerful self, wearing one of Rebecca's dresses, the one with pink polka dots and a massive grey bow across the waist, another favorite item that Jordan had gotten for his wife.

"Good morning," Mandy titters as she glances towards Jordan, who is guzzling his fourth cup of coffee. It's lukewarm but he doesn't seem to notice.

"Are my children up?" Jordan asks, knowing they have not been down yet.

She begins making breakfast and readying the children's lunches.

He had tried to check on his children during the night but couldn't. Mandy had been sprawled on their mattress that she had pulled into the hall and placed in front of the children's room.

Just then, the patter of children running down the steps invades the kitchen. A look of relief passes over Jordan's face. They are dressed in their school clothes and have their backpacks with them.

"You're wearing Mommy's dress," Trevor says, and Jordan takes note that this is the first time one of the kids seems concerned.

"It fits like a glove," Mandy says as she kneels to his eye level. "You know what," she says to him.

"What?" Trevor's eyes widen.

"Your mommy wears my dresses sometimes too. We're like sisters that way."

"You know what," Jordan tries to distract his son. "I don't feel like going to work today. I'll just drop off the kids and…"

Mandy cuts him short with sudden movement as she puts a hand on his forehead. Jordan recoils in disgust.

"You're fine, don't be such a baby! We don't want unwelcome attention now, do we?" She pinches his cheek before turning to face the children.

"Is Mom coming home today?" Cyndi asks hopefully.

"Unlikely," Mandy snaps, but then she regains her composure. "You know that your mother is a very busy person. But I am sure that she misses every one of you terribly. She will be home as soon as she's able." Mandy smiles reassuringly.

"Now, kids, give your father and I a hug before you leave. You will be walking to school this morning and back after school." The kids are staring at their dad as they give Mandy awkward hugs.

They then hug their father as they look at him oddly.

"Do as she says, kids," Jordan cracks a smile. "I love you both so much."

"Love you too, Daddy," Trevor responds.

"Love you," Cyndi mumbles.

"Be good, kids," Mandy says. "Have some Moore fun! A Cure for your Coeur!"

Jordan and the kids freeze, staring at her.

"That's what Mom says on her videos!" Cyndi remarks.

"Are you a fan?" Trevor asks innocently. "Do you like our photos and videos?"

Jordan glowers.

Mandy blushes. "Came across it a couple of times. Who hasn't? That line just stuck with me, I guess."

"Let's go!" Jordan chimes in.

Both Mandy and Jordan watch the kids leave the house, Jordan feeling a bit of relief wash over him. He needs the kids away from her while he figures things out.

"What was that?" Jordan turns to Mandy.

"Nothing. Like I said, catchy line. You know, like a song that's way overplayed, even if you don't like it, it stays in your mind for a while."

Jordan grunts and looks away.

"Now, dear," Mandy says with a grin. "Give Mama a kiss before you head to work. Oh, and the same goes to you…home by six, kids best STAY at school all day! No monkey business!"

Jordan quickly brushes his lips against her cheek, then heads to his room to get ready for work. A few minutes later, he returns downstairs and puts his shoes on, his briefcase by his side.

"Don't forget this," Mandy says.

When Jordan turns around to face her, she is holding the salmon-colored tie she had gotten him the day before. She walks up to him and puts the tie around his neck, taking her time to tie and straighten it. Like she's savoring the moment. She is deliberately being more handsy than needed. Goosebumps swarm his skin every time they touch.

Her hands trail down the tie to the tail that lay just above his belt. She hooks her fingers in his belt and pulls him close.

"I won't do anything stupid," Jordan mutters as he jerks away from her and walks out the door, ready to start the worst day of his life.

*   *   *

After getting in his car, Jordan follows the kids to school without them knowing it. He wants to make sure they make it...they indeed do. Now, he is heading somewhere else, but it isn't work.

He drives a few blocks away from the house, then parks somewhere between the house and where the kids go to school, but off the road enough that Mandy won't notice the car if she comes past.

Instead of going to work, Jordan places a call to work.

"Hi, this is Jordan Moore," he begins to leave a voice message to human resources. "I'm not feeling well today and will be off. Please use my paid leave to cover today. Thank you."

Quickly he gets out of his car. In the trunk, he has a casual outfit tucked away for when he goes to the gym on his lunch hour. He quickly changes into the clothes in his backseat, a shirt, shorts, tennis shoes and a baseball cap. He then opens his briefcase. Instead of folders, there are water bottles scattered in it. He spills everything onto the passenger seat. One of the bottles is empty; he can't afford to take his attention off the house, she may step out any second. He stuffs his dress clothes into his briefcase. His body is rigid with nervousness, his eyes trained on the house like a hawk.

Jordan clings to the thought that he has nothing to worry about. He prays that Mandy won't take chances by calling his work to make sure he is there. She isn't crazy enough to check; they would know it wasn't his wife. His co-workers know her well, they have been to many dinner parties at their house.

Several hours pass without incident. He's down to his last bottle of water. Two of the bottles are filled with yellow, cloudy liquid. He yawns, the fifth time in the last ten minutes.

Then suddenly, there she is. He almost chokes while gulping down some water. Mandy exits the house and unsuspectingly sashays down the road towards the town center.

Jordan lowers his cap and slouches down in his seat. She walks past his car on the other side of the street, not even looking in his direction. Jordan puts on a pair of sunglasses from the dashboard and steps out of the car. He follows her to the main street.

A few blocks later, she stops by a convenience store, and he waits outside. What feels like an hour later, Mandy comes back out with a brown bag, chewing on an apple. Jordan wonders if it is supplies for Rebecca.

Taking her own sweet time, Mandy window shops at a few of the small boutiques, admiring the displays in the window. Jordan is so focused on her that he fails to notice a man standing close to his left, trying to get his attention.

"Excuse me, sir!" a mangy-looking man in a tattered t-shirt blares. "Spare an old man some change?"

Jordan jumps out of his skin and quickly looks in the direction that Mandy had been shopping. To his horror, she looks directly at him and the homeless man. But she seems to immediately lose interest and goes back to the shop's window display. He's praying that she didn't recognize him with the getup.

Jordan turns back to the old man. "Not today, go bother someone else." He says this without contempt, just out of desperation.

"What about a ciggy?" the man asks through a mouth full of crooked and yellowing teeth.

Jordan becomes impatient as the man continues his banter.

"Just…get lost!" he exclaims. He looks at the store again. Mandy is gone. He quickly looks around, scanning the people on the street; she is nowhere to be seen.

He panics and goes into the store.

"Did a woman with dirty blonde hair, middle-aged, come in here? Is she in here now?" Jordan whispers to the man behind the counter.

"There's no one else in the store," the clerk answers. "Man, are you okay? You're sweating something awful."

Without replying, Jordan goes back outside and paces up and down the block. Mandy has vanished without a trace.

Jordan storms in the direction of the homeless man. He grabs the man's dirty t-shirt from behind and pulls him closer. A pungent smell violates his nostrils.

"Are you with her?" Jordan demands.

"What?" the man asks with a look on his face that suggests confusion.

"Did she pay you to distract me? A guy like you would do anything for money, right?"

"I don't know what you talkin' 'bout, pal," the man says, with fear in his eyes now.

"You're crazy to think I believe that in the least," Jordan says.

"What in the hell," the homeless guy says as he pulls on the hold Jordan has on him.

"I said you are crazy. Were you helping the bitch? Tell me now or I will…"

"Help!" The man's shout cuts him off. "This man is harassing me! Please!"

Everyone is looking at them, forcing Jordan to let go of his grip. Frustrated, he scans the street once more. Not seeing anything of interest, he sprints away back to his car, knowing the kids will be out of school any minute.

*　　*　　*

Jordan returns to his car just in time to see the kids come down the road. For a moment, he thinks about sweeping them up and getting away…going to the cops, even, but that could mean he may never see Rebecca again.

He's still debating the best course of action as they are coming across the intersection towards the house. Jordan opens the door of his car and starts to step out but then sees Mandy meet them in the middle of the road.

She says something to them, but Jordan can't make out what they are talking about. Sliding back into the car, he closes the door silently. He watches as Mandy puts her hand on Cynthia's shoulder. Trevor walks in front of them as it looks like Mandy is pushing Cyndi along.

Once the kids are out of sight, Jordan starts his car and heads away from the house. He needs Mandy to believe he has been at work, so he has about two and a half hours to kill until he can get home.

He drives for a bit before parking in the country. Jordan pulls his briefcase back out and gets dressed again, making sure to put the tie back on for good measure.

Ring, ring!

His cell sounds off at a quarter to five.

"Hello," Jordan says after recognizing the number.

"Hey, this is Suzan from HR, your wife's friend from school," the woman on the other line says, and Jordan realizes it is in fact someone from his work.

"How can I help you, Suzan?" Jordan asks. "Did you get my call this morning?"

"We did," Susan says on the other line. "But that's not why I'm calling."

"Oh, okay," Jordan says. "So, what's up?"

"Your wife called a few minutes ago," Suzan says.

"My wife, are you sure?"

"Absolutely," her voice sounds chipper. "We hadn't talked in a few months, it was nice to hear from her. She wanted me to call you, said your cell hadn't been working all day, and when I said you called in sick, she seemed to be surprised."

"And you know it was Becs?" Jordan asks again. "There is a woman trying to act as my wife."

"Nope, this was Rebecca. Uhm...at least I thought so. She said you should head home. That your kids are going to need you." She paused for a moment. "You know, Jordan, if you have a woman trying to be your wife, you should really report it to the police."

"Forget what I said, it's been taken care of," Jordan says, putting the car into drive. "Nice to talk to you, Suzan, maybe we can have you over soon," he finishes, then he hangs up and begins to drive full speed towards town.

Less than fifteen minutes later, Jordan returns home. He runs into the house hoping that somehow Rebecca is there. Without even stopping, he goes to the kitchen, then the living room, upstairs, each bedroom…nothing. The kids and Mandy are nowhere to be seen.

Jordan does, however, find one thing odd. The master bathroom has what looks like blood on the sink. He is afraid to look any further, but he must investigate. He walks inside and is quickly angered and relieved at the same time.

In the trash is a box of red hair dye…it's everywhere. It looks like a messy massacre.

Around the two-hour mark, and about the time he would normally be getting home from work, Jordan begins pacing nervously in the living room, biting his nails.

He had considered calling the cops many times since coming home but is holding out. He doesn't want to risk his family any more by getting the authorities involved. After another hour, he gets as far as pressing 9 on his phone and hanging up repeatedly.

The second he keys in the 9 and the first 1, a clearly red-headed Mandy and the kids come through the door.

Jordan turns his phone off and rushes to his kids. He wraps his arms around them and hugs them as though he hasn't seen them in years.

"Where did you guys go?" he asks, trying to sound as calm as possible.

"Mandy took us to Galaxy Pizza," Trevor said with joy in his voice. "You and Mom never let us go there."

"We came home, she dyed her hair, then she told us you said

we could go," Cyndi adds, her voice unsteady.

"That's right, Daddy just forgot is all," Jordan offers a smile. "Now, why don't you guys go up and get cleaned up for the night."

"Can I play on my Nintendo Switch?" Trevor asks.

"Of course, you can," Mandy says, causing Trevor to then look at his father.

"For an hour before bed," he agrees. "But make sure to shower and brush your teeth first."

Jordan watches as his kids run up the steps.

"Hope you're not hungry, I didn't get you anything," Mandy leers, as the kids finish their climb and disappear around the corner.

Jordan can tell she's extremely upset. She stands with her arms crossed, scowling at him.

"Are you going to say anything about my hair?" Mandy asks, her arms still crossed. There's a twinkle in her eye.

"It's nice," Jordan replies dryly. His nose can't help but wrinkle. "Rebecca's natural red is preferable though," he adds, hoping it comes as a blow to her.

She glares at him. "I was this close to ending this all... because of your stupidity," she admits through gritted teeth and clenched jaws.

"I know I messed up, but my work says that Rebecca called... was it her, or you?" He's hoping Mandy won't know anything about that.

"That prep-school wannabe bought my old schoolmate routine...hook...line...and sinker," Mandy says, blowing on her fingertips as though drying newly polished nails.

"I really need to see her; you can't possibly understand. Can I talk to her? I have to know if she's okay," Jordan says, trying to play to her softer side.

"You wanna see her? I'll do you one better," she says as she pulls something out from her folded arms.

Mandy tosses him something.

He catches it. Letting out a shriek, he drops it. Strands of red hair banded by an elastic. Lying lifelessly on the floor.

"You try to be a hero again, it will be more than just her hair you'll be getting," Mandy threatens.

Jordan is lost. He gets on his knees as he picks up and clutches the strands of hair, sniffling and fighting back tears. His hands are trembling.

"I love you, Becs," he whispers, praying that she knows it. He's holding on to the strands of hair as if they were his most prized possession.

"You can have your bed tonight. I think you've learned your lesson," Mandy tosses her new auburn hair and wheels away.

*   *   *

Jordan thought it would be impossible to fall asleep. Eventually he did. But he's restless, drifting in and out of sleep. Each time, he feels that Rebecca is lying next to him. But when he looks, the space next to him is cold and empty.

Something awakens him sometime in the morning. The first thing he sees is an outline of a head crowned with a red bush of hair.

Becs, you're finally back…

He jolts, realizing that it isn't her. Mandy. She is sitting down on the bedside chair…her head is just inches away from his. Jordan jerks away in shock. He sits up rigidly in the dark of his room.

"What…what do you want? Are you watching me sleep?"

Mandy just smirks, her eyes distant. She puts a hand on his chest. At once Jordan pushes it away.

"Don't be like that. We're both adults here," Mandy says in a sultry voice…the want heavy there.

Jordan looks utterly terrified and disgusted, clutching the bedsheet.

"Get…the fuck…out of my bedroom," he fumes.

"Playing hard to get, I see," Mandy teases as she stands up, only wearing a sheer gown. "If you ever wanna see her again…" She trails off as she leans over to put her hands on the bed, showing a great deal of cleavage.

This can't be happening. Jordan isn't ready to rule out the fact that he's having a nightmare, or that he's in hell. In the dark, he can feel his back and neck slick with sweat. His forehead is throbbing and his mouth is as dry as an old man's sac in a sauna. Then it hits him. *This is real. She is not an illusion.*

"Stay—the fuck away!"

"What you have to know is," Mandy begins as she crawls a tad closer. "Is that I'm a very dangerous woman. And you have no idea what I could do to your precious little wifey. Not to mention those precious angels."

"You're certifiably insane!" Jordan pushes his back up against the headboard. "You need help!"

"You think I'm crazy?" It's more of a statement rather than a question. "That's right. You haven't met my partner, have you?"

"Partner?" Jordan raises an eyebrow, shrinking away.

"Yeah," she says as she moves even closer. "He's the insane

one, jealous too. With just a call, I'd unleash him on your beautiful wife. He's with her now, you know." She straightens up and begins to slip off the straps of her gown. One at a time. "Oh…God…" she moans dramatically with a hand to her forehead. "Oh, he's such a swine! Things he's made me do for him!"

The upper part of her gown peels away, revealing a set of perky tits. Jordan grimaces, the room is beginning to spin. He can't tell if she is telling the truth or bluffing, which makes her even more dangerous than he once thought.

"What is it you want? I can pay you," Jordan mumbles, but Mandy only comes closer, eyes trained on him. Like a leopard to a cornered gazelle.

"You…I want you, Jordan," she whispers as she touches his face.

Jordan flinches, but her hands are on his shoulder, slowly moving down his arms to his fingers.

"I…I…" Jordan stammers.

"You don't know how long I've dreamed of this," she interrupts.

Jordan's face and body are as inflexible as Madame Tussaud's wax sculptures. With both hands, she moves his tense body to one side, making him lie down on the bed, right where Rebecca should be sleeping soundly in his arms.

Mandy pulls down his boxers as his body grows even stiffer…his muscles are so drawn he feels like he has just come off a marathon.

"Don't look so glum, handsome. Trust me, you gonna like this," Mandy murmurs as Jordan feels his maleness in her hands.

"Don't," he says, but it's so quiet, he isn't sure he even made a sound.

"I need you to want me like you want her," Mandy demands, her lips moist and slightly parted. Suddenly her face disappears. Then he feels wetness. And tugging.

Jordan clenches his fists and jaw. He can feel a rising bile in his throat as he shuts both eyes tightly.

*   *   *

The next day, after calling in yet again, and long after he knows the children have made it to school, Jordan comes home.

He marches through the house looking for the bitch who has taken over his life. He finds her in his bedroom, sitting on the bed, her back resting against the headboard like she belongs there.

He's carrying a gym bag with him. There's steely determination in his eyes when he notices Mandy is knitting one of the projects Rebecca had been working on. She is sitting in the exact spot where the unspeakable thing took place the night before. Out of nowhere, she bursts out laughing, throwing her head back and finishing it off with a little snort.

He realizes that she's watching Rebecca's favorite TV show. Jordan feels a little lightheaded. With violent, snapping movements, Jordan unzips the bag and hurls it onto the bed beside her.

"There's ten thousand dollars in there, I can get you more," he declares.

"Whatever for?" Mandy continues to work on the project, never turning her eyes from the show.

"Give her back and get out of our lives!" Jordan raises his voice. "We will never tell a soul anything."

"You don't get it, do you?" she says, turning his way for the first time since he walked in the room. "I don't want money, Jordan. That was never the intention."

"Then what the hell do you want?"

"Where are the kids!" Mandy screams, ignoring him. There was a genuine concern in her voice.

"I dropped them off someplace safe," he offers.

Mandy looks at him with hurt in her eyes.

"Safe from what, Jordan?" she asks, glowering.

"I just don't want them anywhere near this house until the situation is resolved," Jordan explains. "Don't take it personally."

"Anywhere near me, you mean?" A darkness enshrouds her face.

Jordan stays silent.

"You've got no right!" Mandy screeches. "They need me! You think I would hurt them?" Her eyes are wide open. "I know I have made you worry, but I wouldn't touch them. I love them. Those were just empty threats to get you to cooperate!"

"They need their REAL mom!" Jordan bellows. "Not some psycho-bitch-slash-kidnapper who holds them hostage."

Mandy drops what she is doing and stands up. She's wearing another one of Rebecca's dresses. It's the yellow one with sunflowers on it. Jordan can't place where or when his wife had gotten this one, though he remembers her wearing it on many occasions. A single tear runs down the side of her face.

She looks enraged and defiant.

She snatches a purse that Jordan immediately recognizes as Rebecca's from the nightstand and storms in the direction of the front door. Jordan grabs her arm to stop her. She spins around and faces him. Her face is contorting as if it's full of ants crawling just under the epidermis. Jordan almost does not recognize her.

"I warned you!" She spits out the words with fury.

"They will be back," Jordan stammers. "I promise."

It isn't a total lie; he had called his parents to pick the kids up after school and hold onto them until it was safe. His folks didn't even ask why. Of course, he didn't tell them the reason or that his wife was missing, or that some psycho bitch was holding them hostage, but he figured he would do that when the time is right.

"Too late, it's over!" Mandy says as she lifts her chin high.

"I'm sorry," Jordan backtracks. "I didn't mean what I said. Look, I just need to do some thinking about us. About you. How…how we can function as a…a…big, happy family." He tries hard to cool her jets.

Mandy sneers as she pulls her arm free and keeps walking. Jordan is desperate at this point. He grabs her arm again.

"Where are you going? What are you gonna do exactly?" he pleads, trying to get anything out of her.

He now realizes that the situation has flipped. When he went into the house, he thought he would have the upper hand, but now Mandy clearly does. He hadn't figured this scenario in, but now that it's happening, he doesn't know what to do, other than beg.

"Oh, trust me," Mandy leans in to whisper into Jordan's ear. "You don't want to know."

"Tell me what that means." Jordan refuses to let go of her arm. "You're not gonna hurt her, are you?"

Mandy struggles to get her arm free, to no avail. Jordan is sure she knows he won't hurt her for the same reason he knows he won't.

"Hurt her?" Mandy finally says. "Never said that she's still alive!" She purrs in hushed tones. "She's probably a half-dead rag doll in a ditch somewhere by now!"

Jordan loses his mind. He grabs her by the neck, dragging her back into the living room. All he sees is red.

"Help! Help!" Mandy screams between wheezing breaths.

"Yeah, let it out, girl, hopefully someone will call the cops," Jordan hisses, his mind gone in grief and anger. "Something I should've done sooner."

Those words shut her up. Jordan quickly scans the room. He shuffles sideways, dragging Mandy's body. With one hand on Mandy's neck, he extends his other arm to reach a hanging shelf above a side table. Out of a metal can, he pulls out a pair of scissors.

In desperation, Mandy sinks her teeth into his arm. Jordan yelps and reflexively punches her in the back of the head. She's momentarily dazed. Jordan lifts her up and lumbers forward. After a few steps, he hurls Mandy facedown on the couch and pins her down with his own body weight, lying prone atop of her.

He then places the sharp edge of a shear of the scissors to Mandy's carotid.

"You better start talking, bitch!" Jordan mutters as he presses the blade against her neck.

"Ow!" Mandy shrieks as Jordan draws a trickle of blood from below the blade.

"Where's my wife?" He's made up his mind to extract information from her no matter what.

He holds one of her hands down and pricks her skin even more with the tip of the scissors. This time deeper, twisting the end ever so slightly.

"Stop," Mandy pleads.

"Where is she?" Jordan yells at a squirming Mandy as spittle showers her face. "Next, the blade is going into your eyeball!" He grabs her head and pulls it back. With the other hand, he guides the scissors towards her left eye. She is resisting like hell. But the protruding point keeps coming closer. It is now dangerously near her eyeball. Then it's even closer, almost touching.

Ding! Ding! The doorbell rings, startling Jordan. The scissors drop to the floor. He reaches down to the side to retrieve them.

Using his momentum, Mandy topples his body over, hitting the ground. Mandy jolts up and runs for the door. As Jordan gets to his feet, Mandy has grabbed the door handle and is turning it. She flings it open and dashes out.

Phil from next door is standing outside. He must have heard some noise and is now watching Mandy run away, blood dripping down her neck.

The man's eyes quickly turn to him. Utter confusion is written all over his face.

*   *   *

It took some fast talking for Jordan to get himself out of a mess. After talking with the children, the police deemed the incident as self-defense. They now have an APB out for Mandy, although they don't have a last name. The police have been searching the house for clues and trying frantically to locate Mandy, but so far there has been nothing. Search and rescue have been looking for Rebecca Moore. But no luck, not even a single useful lead.

Jordan glances at his phone for the tenth time as he pulls up outside his house. It is the first time he or the children had returned other than to get their clothes. He, the kids, and his parents have been living at a hotel for a few days now. Out of the blue, an hour earlier, he got a text from Rebecca's number, telling him to come back to the house. Afraid that he might lose courage, Jordan hurriedly gets out of the car and approaches the house.

He's armed. He knows he should've told the police about the text but decided against it at the last minute. He thought that the cops would just complicate things and may get in the way, should he choose to end things his way. Most importantly, he felt the need to get to the bottom of things personally. But now that he's here, it all sounds stupid and lame, suicidal even.

He didn't even tell his parents or the kids what was up. He had just told them that he was running some errands.

He's hoping to see his wife more than anything. But if the bitch Mandy is there instead, or her "crazy partner," he intends to shed some blood.

The door to the house is slightly ajar. With great hesitation, he holds up the gun like he had done all those years at the gun range. Watching people go into a house with a gun on television is nothing like doing it in person. Especially when you don't know what you're facing and what's on the line.

He scrambles inside with a gulp.

Inside, the house looks exactly like how he left it the last time. Except for one thing. In all the family pictures around the house, in the entryway, living room, and up the banister to the steps, Rebecca's face has been aggressively covered by black ink marks or scratched out with a knife. His hands tighten around the gun handle. His face is sickly pale and sweaty.

Jordan cautiously checks the rest of the ground floor and finds nothing else of interest. But on the coffee table is his wife's cell phone.

He goes straight to it and picks it up. He unlocks the phone while keeping diligent watch of his surroundings. His back is to a wall while he faces the only two entrances to the house. The back door through the kitchen is in front of him, and the foyer is to his right.

After unlocking the phone, he brings the phone closer to his face. The display on the screen is on WordPad. It looks like a letter.

Dear Jordan,

I know that you want to hurt me badly and be rid of me. But I need to tell you my story. It's possible you don't care at this point, but if you want to learn about your wife, then read on.

Jordan lowers the phone. He's got a really bad feeling about this. But he doesn't have any choice. This is the only way to find out. He takes several deep breaths and returns his gaze to the phone.

Once, I led a normal, happy life. I had a loving husband whom I adored, a little mischievous boy who loved yo-yos and chewing gum, and a beautiful girl with dimpled cheeks and freckled arms who was starting to look at boys with a little too much interest. I'd do anything for them. I was on top of the world as their mother, as his wife.

One night, we were driving home from the cinema. My husband was in the driver's seat, and I was beside him. The kids had fallen asleep in the backseat as they were probably dreaming of dragons and princesses, their little hands and breaths smelling of buttery popcorn.

Roy was his usual silly self, trying to turn the movie we just watched into a comedy by substituting actors and imagining what they would do. "Just My Imagination" was playing softly through the radio.

Roy said that he'd like to see Joe Pesci as the priest, and I failed miserably at subduing the laughter that was exploding inside me. It came out sounding like the barks of a choking dog, drowning Dolores O'Riordan's lilting voice in the background.

One second everything's right with the world and the next, some drunk trucker destroyed everything I ever cared for and loved…

After their deaths, I was a total wreck, hating everything and everyone. Above all, I condemned myself. I was repulsed by my own reflection, recoiled by my own touch. Why? Why couldn't I just have died with them? Why am I left alone in this unfeeling world?

Believe me, I have tried to end it myself numerous times. But all that just took me to a darker place. I was neither living nor dead.

Then something brought me back from the brink of hell.

It was your family's vlog.

It was like I woke from a coma. I found a reason to get up in the morning, to overcome my anguish. A reason to live. The show became a big part of my being, my solace. I lived my family through yours.

For a while, that was enough. Then one day a thought struck me; what if there's a way to have it all, the real deal.

All I wanted was to feel once again those lost feelings of belonging, of being wanted, loved. And most of all, the feeling of having something to hold dear, to lose.

If the few days with you and the kids have taught me anything, it's that the salvation I was seeking does not exist. It's a mirage in this cold, cruel world.

Lovingly, now, and always,

Mandy

P.S. Sorry about the mess.

P.P.S. About the wife: It wouldn't be fair for someone to have everything while the other is reduced to a mere fragment of existence, forever abandoned and in tatters.

Jordan seethes with rage, tasting blood. What does that mean? A train of thoughts race through his mind as he looks up from the phone. He begins to hastily search the house, hoping to find something. *Sorry for the mess.* Did she leave him a surprise somewhere in the house?

The ground floor is empty…nothing, not even a clue other than the pictures and the phone. He then heads upstairs and enters the master bedroom. There, Mandy is hung from the ceiling, a knotted necktie around her neck…the salmon one she had gotten him. He had left it in the trash bin in the master bath.

Her lifeless body swings gently, seemingly following the rhythm of the humming of the rotating ceiling fan. Mandy is wearing Rebecca's wedding gown. And her wedding ring too. Jordan is rooted to the ground. He has just lost his only clue as to Rebecca's whereabouts. And if his wife is still alive. Then there is the end of the letter…

Then he sees it. A long necklace lops below her breasts. A singular pendant sits just above her navel. From the doorway, it looks like a seashell.

Jordan comes closer, as he lets the gun hang to his side. Then it falls to the ground.

The pendant is no seashell at all. It's an ear.

A hole has been put through the top. A singular string was pierced through it.

But it's the identifying feature that brings Jordan to his knees.

On the lobe of the ear, sits a gold earring. With a teardrop dangle.

EN PRISE

A Budweiser bottle screams past my head. I follow its trajectory as if it's in slow-mo. The dark amber hue of the glass seems to be changing opacity as it floats across the room. What little liquid remains in the bottle sloshes about like little waves on the shore of a deserted island. A few drips of glossy, sun-bleached bubbles make it out, suspended in midair. At first it looks like the bottle is going to smash into the small window on the far wall, but it deftly dips down at the last second and dives into a wide tin bucket, joining several other wrecked bottles. There is an ear-piercing chorus of shattering glass. Practice makes perfect.

Dex is at it again. He came home in a rage, flung the door of the trailer open wide, almost ripping it off its hinges.

I look up from my coffee as he storms in, cussing, stomping his feet like some water buffalo, and making a beeline to the old refrigerator buzzing in the corner of the kitchen. I watch in silence, waiting for the eruption. When he is in one of these moods, there's no way of dragging him out of it. I just have to wait it out and hope that not too many things get trashed.

He roams the room, a lanky figure dressed in an old flannel shirt, slip-on sneakers with creases, shabby jean shorts cut unevenly.

His ponytail swings agitatedly behind him. A frown wrinkles his high forehead. His lips are pressed tightly together.

As expected, he scurries to where the drinks are. Dex kicks the fridge and immediately swears at it for hurting his toe. Then he opens its door and grabs his fourth beer at ten in the morning. He turns around to face me. There's a sneer on his face, daring me to criticize, to say anything. I sit unmoving at the tiny kitchen table, holding my coffee cup as if it will somehow protect me.

He shouts, "Why the hell don't you get that stupid thing fixed?" He uses one hand to pop the cap off the beer bottle by banging it against the edge of the kitchen table. The beer cap flies to the ground. He drains half the bottle in one gulp.

I stare at him. "Cut that out, Dex. You've done enough damage to this table as it is, and it's not a damn beer bottle opener." I immediately regret saying this but can't help myself. I have had just about enough of his bullshit.

He stands still with that stupid grin on his face and slowly finishes his beer, his eyes zeroed in on me. He belches noisily and then abruptly whips the empty bottle in my direction.

I can hear it cutting through the air, just missing my ear and smashing into a million pieces in the sink filled with dirty dishes behind me.

That is it. I jump up, my coffee cup toppling onto the floor, and the brown liquid running onto the worn linoleum. "Asshole!" I shout. "What the fuck is the matter with you! Loser!" My face grows hot, and every muscle in my body is wound tight as I try to make myself look big in front of him. Dex is taller than me, but kind of scrawny.

He leers at me, rubbing the five-o'clock shadow on his chin.

"Loser, huh? What does that make you, then?"

I shake my head. We've been together for two tumultuous years. When we first met I thought he was kinda cute. A wild, reckless guy who looked pretty hot on his custom Harley.

One day he walked into the body shop where I worked, wearing the same red plaid shirt and jeans he'd had on for the last three days, his black motorcycle boots covered in mud. He asked me out then and there, a tomboy apprentice in oil-splattered coveralls, in front of the guys. I was blushing from head to toe but my heart was giddy with anticipation. I felt special. This wild-looking cowboy from nowhere, barging in the way he did, just to be with me. There was a time when I genuinely thought that I loved him. We had some laughs and adventures, but as the months went on, the bad times quickly outnumbered the good ones.

At that very moment, as I prop myself in the puddle of spilled coffee, I know that it's over. Dex scratches his nose. "You're the loser, Ash, you and your stupid guitar. You think you're gonna be the next Ani DiFranco? What a joke. You'll be working at the Stellar Dollar for the rest of your life."

"You're a dick, Dex," I reply, pretending that his words don't cut me to the bone. "At least I have a job."

Dex ambles closer to me, his nose almost touching mine. I can smell his beer breath, but I refuse to step back. We lock eyes. Those once-beautiful green eyes of his are now bloodshot and dull. He sneers, "I don't need this from you. Stop judging me, bitch!" I hold my position, determined to not back down first. I don't know what to expect from him next. Will he slap me around, push me backward onto the kitchen table?

He does neither. Dex scoffs and spits on the floor. Then he

storms out of the trailer without saying another word, battering the door on his way out. The whole trailer shakes.

I freeze for a few seconds, but that's all it takes for me to make a decision. It's time to leave this shitty trailer and all this crap behind. My eyes have finally been pried open. This is a road to nowhere. Can't keep on living like this, dying inside a little at a time.

I walk to the bedroom at the other end of the trailer. I pick up my backpack and start to empty the dresser drawers.

Satisfied that all my worldly possessions, which isn't much, are packed, I approach the bed that Dex and I had shared for the last two years. The wooden headboard has "A ♠ D" carved into it. I remember carving it when we first moved in together. Suddenly, rage boils inside me and takes over. I take my pocketknife out and flick open the blade. Without hesitation, I cross out the obsolete proclamation. I step back and nod. It definitely looks much better now.

I sling my backpack over my shoulder, grab my guitar case, and bolt out of the trailer, slamming that flimsy aluminum door after me. Then I stop.

There's Dex, sitting in one of our lawn chairs with two of his deadbeat buddies, Rick and Ethan. My jaw clenches. Dex gawks at me, a cigarette dangling from his lips. Crushed butts and empty beer bottles surround him like some white-trash shrine. Rick and Ethan stand idly, drinking and smoking. They stare at the backpack and the guitar case. Then back to me. Their eyes are bright with anticipation. They know juicy drama when they see it, this place is full of it, twenty-four-seven.

Dex spouts, "What do you think you're doing?"

I snap, "What I should've done a long time ago. I'm sick and tired of your shit!" There, I say it, about time.

Dex looks at his buddies. "You boys hear that?" He gulps down some beer. He wipes his mouth with the dirty sleeve of his shirt. "Fuckin' unbelievable! After everything I've done for this bitch?!" Rick and Ethan snigger.

I stare at Dex with chin held high. "What exactly have you done for me? What have you done with your fucking life, Dex? Achieved anything? Learned anything?" I know what the real answer is.

Dex glares at me, slumped in that tattered lawn chair. He opens his mouth, but nothing comes out. What I said must have shocked him.

"Precisely!" I remark.

Ethan and Rick started to snigger again. Dex shoots them a pissy look and they immediately clam up. He pulls himself out of the chair, a bit unsteady after the amount of beer he has consumed. He points at me with his index finger. "Watch your mouth, you ungrateful little…"

I'm not letting him finish. I just turn away and walk towards my car.

He is silent for a few seconds, probably isn't expecting how the situation has turned out. "Don't come back and beg me to forgive your sorry ass. I'm fucking done with you. You're nothing but bad luck!" I can hear hesitation in his voice; moron thinks he's tough. Flicking him the finger, I stomp to my car, an old Toyota sedan with paint peeling off the hood.

Dex carries on, near-screaming now, "I don't know what I saw in you. Ugly as a donkey's ass, can't cook for shit. And a lousy lay to boot!"

Curious faces begin peering out from behind curtains and doors. I open the back passenger door of my car, throw my backpack in, and place my guitar case on the backseat.

That dumbass Rick has to add his two cents, of course. "Ugly-ass pussy beats jerking off, in my opinion."

Ethan chimes in, "No one asked you, jerk! But I'd do'er, as long as she keeps that piehole shut and looks the other way." The sound of their cackling makes my skin crawl. Imagine a pack of howling hyenas, stalking their prey. It's bizarre that they sound almost identical and in sync when they cackle. Never thought of it before, but they must hold regular practices or something, like an a capella group. The silliness of that idea calms me down plenty. Then Dex starts calling me every name under the sun. A last-ditch effort to bring me down to their level.

I get into the driver's seat and put the key in the ignition. Giving Dex and his two loser friends one last glance, I gun the engine and speed off down the gravel road, kicking up enough dust and dirt to blot out the view of their hideous faces in my rear-view mirror.

*　*　*

I keep going all night, only stopping a couple of times on the interstate for gas and to grab some Cokes and use the toilet. I drive in silence, not bothering to turn on the crappy radio that came with my Toyota. After the kind of day I just had, some quiet is in order. Feeling so weary from years of yelling and fighting with Dex, I welcome the solitude whenever I can. When Dex and his clones aren't around, I play my guitar outside the trailer. Under the naked sky. It has been my ultimate pleasure and solace.

I'm free, and once again single. But that doesn't matter now, I need a break. It's such a huge relief to not have to be constantly looking over my shoulder or waiting for the next fight. All the emotional roller-coaster that was me and Dex is now lifted. As far as I'm concerned, he can drink himself to death. I don't think he'd follow me, just too lazy to do that. At least I hope so. Anyway, the more miles I put between me and Dex, the better.

I think about stopping at a motel for the night but realize that there's less than $100 in my purse and I'll need it for gas. There's the credit card, but it's maxed out, so it's essentially useless. Without much choice, I soldier on, past two state lines, and back to my home state.

At around midnight, I pull up in front of my mom's bungalow. I've been driving for about twelve hours straight now. I stop the car, turn off the engine, and take in the familiar house, illuminated by an anemic streetlight. When I stormed out on Dex, there wasn't any grand plan, but to somehow end up in front of my mom's house…it's as if I drove in a trance back to here. Just like salmon, they always come back to the stream where it all started. Suddenly, I feel an overwhelming wave of exhaustion.

I grab my backpack and guitar case, walk up to the house, climb the familiar red brick steps, and knock on the door. And another. A light comes on upstairs, and shortly in the front hall and the porch. I call out, "Mom, it's me, Ash."

Mom answers, her voice muffled, coming from the other side of the front door. "Ash? Ash, is that you?" She is probably looking at me through the security peephole in the door but not quite believing her eyes. I grin and wave at the peephole.

"It's me, Mama, I'm sorry it's so late." I feel so stupid, knocking on her door in the middle of the night. Mom unlocks the door, and it slowly swings open. And there she is, holding onto the doorknob. She peeks her head around the door, squinting in the low light. I haven't seen her in months, and there are at least a few more grey hairs on her head. She is wearing her pink housecoat, which she's had for years, and a pair of fuzzy white slippers.

"Ash, it's you!" Mom gasps. Then she hugs me warmly. "Come in, let's go to the kitchen, I'll make some tea." She gives me a big hug and motions me to follow her inside. I drop my gear by the front door and follow her to the kitchen. Mom puts the kettle on. I stand next to the ancient Formica kitchen table that has been in my earliest memories growing up.

"Ash, is something wrong? You didn't call that you were coming. Everything alright?" Her hair is a bit disheveled from sleep, but being Mom, she senses that something is off.

I decide to play it cool. "Nothing's wrong, Mom, just missing you is all."

Mom is studying me, the way she looks at me when catching me in a lie. She doesn't argue, just calmly waits for the kettle to start to boil and whistle. She turns off the burner, grabs two mugs and a couple of teabags, and places them on the table.

That's when I lose it. The simple act of Mom making tea at midnight somehow opens the floodgates. Tears start to flow from my eyes. Mom walks over and I just fall into her warm embrace. I sob like a fifteen-year-old who's had her heart broken the first time, crying into Mom's prominent bosom. I let out everything. About my fight with Dex, our breakup. And then the conversation descends into a pity party, admitting to her that I feel like an utter failure. Mom just holds me there for the entire time, letting me spill my guts, our tea getting cold.

"Ash," Mom whispers gently. "You're much stronger than you think. We survived him, we can handle anything. You will weather this storm and get your life together."

The *him* she's referring to is an old lover. She had fallen hard and fast for his handsome face and dark eyes, but he turned out to be an abusive degenerate.

I nod, sipping some lukewarm tea, and wipe away tears with the back of my hand. Mom sits down next to me, her hands on my knees. "You need Dex like an elephant needs a diary." I laugh. It feels good. What would I do without her?

"Mom," I say, sniffling and trying to clear my throat. "I'm thinking of visiting my old friend Lauren, you know, the musician from Rockwood?"

"Oh yes, I remember her. She's such a wonderful girl, so talented." Mom offers me a big smile and squeezes my knees. I can tell she is glad that I left Dex.

"A few months ago, she offered to share her apartment with me, if I ever decided to leave here. She's been indirectly telling me to dump Dex for so long. Should've listened to her the first time."

"Better late than never," Mom quips.

"She also offered to introduce me to her manager, maybe land me some gigs."

"That's wonderful, Ash," Mom replies. "You still play?"

"Here and there, not as much as I'd like," I say.

"This is great. You've always had an ear for music, I hope everything will work out." My mom twinkles, taking a sip of her tea.

We sit and sip for a while. "Ash, let me see your mug." Oh no, here we go again, I think.

"Oh Mom, do I have to?"

"Ash, it'll be fun. Humor me. No charge." Mom winks. "Finish it up, kiddo."

I roll my eyes and glug down my tea. Mom's been reading my fortune since I was a kid, but I've never been a believer. Her readings have always been hit or miss.

Mom takes the cup away from my hand. She brings the opening close to her face and swirls it around. Creasing her brows, she starts to make some noises, like "hmm" and "umm." I know she does this for effect, to keep me in suspense.

"Mom," I say. "So, what do you see? Am I gonna win the lottery soon? Die a miserable death in a ditch?"

Mom scowls at me. "You never take anything seriously, kid. Why would you say things like that?" She looks at me as if I were a child caught red-handed eating cookies right before dinner.

"Please, I'm dying to find out what fate has in store for me! Tell me!" I put my hands together in a praying position, a smirk on my face.

Mom shakes her head in disbelief. Then she begins, "You will soon meet a mysterious stranger that you will develop strong feelings for."

"Is he tall, dark, and handsome? Seven-figure bank account and lives in a castle?" I grin from ear to ear. "Not with his mom, though, that's a deal-breaker!"

Then suddenly the look on my mom's face changes drastically. Her smile fades. It's like a shadow has passed over us.

"I'm kidding, sorry!" I apologize, thinking that my sarcasm

was the reason for the abrupt transformation. She's staring at the leaf trails with empty eyes, no movement. I feel a slight chill.

"Mom, what is it?" I bring my face closer to hers.

"Not sure, to be honest. Your life will take an unexpected turn, Ash, but it's vague. You'll find yourself at a crossroads. I can't really see…"

"Mom, what?" I'm starting to get a little spooked. Mom takes her readings very seriously; it's not just child's play.

Abruptly she drops the cup, as if it was a burning coal. It shatters against the linoleum floor. We look at each other. Eventually she sits up and waves her hands, face flushed. "Oh, it's nothing, dear, I think I may be going a bit senile. I'm sorry, it's nothing." She staggers to the pantry and collects a mini broom and dustpan set.

"Are you sure? Looks like you've seen a ghost," I persist. I take the broom set from her and start to clean up the mess on the floor.

"Love, I'm not even sure what I saw. Just promise me to be careful out there. You can be too trusting and naive sometimes," she pleads.

"I can perfectly take care of my—"

She shushes me, "Just promise me, Ash."

I think about responding to her with something witty but change my mind. There's an immovable graveness in her eyes and voice.

"Okay, Mom, promise."

Mom gets me a new cup and fills both cups with more hot water and tea.

I clutch my teacup, thankful for the warmth and the familiar taste of chamomile and cinnamon. I try to shake off the dread that had briefly come over me during the reading. Mom said that she was getting confused, but I know better. She's sharp as a tack and nothing scares her. She saw something. Hopefully I'll never find out what it was.

*   *   *

We go to bed around midnight. Mom puts me up in my old room. Everything is almost exactly the way I remember it. I think it's funny and sweet that she keeps all my artwork, school photos, and my stuffed animals neatly arranged on a bookcase by the window. My old, faded, unicorn-blue comforter is still on the bed, and the old superhero figurines are all lined up on a shelf above the headboard. Mom turns on the bedside lamp, its yellow light casting a warm glow around the room. I kiss her good night and then change my clothes. I thought about getting a quick shower, but the allure of a warm bed is too strong. The argy-bargy with Dex and the long drive finally catching up with me, I'm entirely spent. I soak up the recognizable smells of my room, the pillow, and the sheets on the bed. Within seconds, I'm fast asleep.

*   *   *

I awake with a start. The sun is just emerging through the bedroom window. Birds are chirping in the huge oak tree in the front yard. Before we went to bed, Mom offered me a ride to the train station. There is a direct train to Rockwood, and it runs daily at nine a.m. Sitting up in bed, I realize that I'm low on cash, no longer thinking that taking the train is a good idea. It would be ideal to take the car, but then I wouldn't get far on the money I have. Choosing not to ask Mom for some, I decide to hitch rides to the city. It's pocket-friendly and a little adventure is long overdue. In order to avoid prolonged arguments with Mom, I opt for the cowardly solution. I will slip out quietly before she wakes up, take a walk to the highway and hitch a ride. I know she would object and most importantly, I loathe saying goodbye. Especially to her.

I quietly visit the toilet. I brush my teeth, wash my face, and put on a clean shirt. After making the bed, I scribble a note, telling Mom that I will be back for my car, then tiptoe to her room. I watch her for a minute, following the rhythmic falling and rising of her chest. She is even snoring a bit. In this moment, I feel so at peace, not a worry in the world. I feel guilty for not staying longer; so many things to be said and done, but I have to keep going. Can't afford to get too comfortable. If not now, probably never. I owe it to myself to see more of the world and be someone with a purpose.

I toddle closer to Mom, who is sleeping soundly on her side, the covers pulled up to her chin. I bend down and kiss her lightly on the forehead, fighting back tears. I put my note on her bedside table and slip downstairs.

Peeking in the kitchen, I notice that Mom had prepared me some surprises, a stack of peanut butter and jelly sandwiches with sliced bananas, my go-to since I can't remember when. Next to the sandwiches is a bag of homemade chocolate-chip cookies, my ultimate childhood fave, a big bottle of water, and an envelope filled with folded bills of twenties.

There's a note on the table, folded in half. I open it, my hands slightly trembling. It reads, "I know u don't do goodbyes. ☺ Take these for the road. Love u to the moon and back my little Koala! Mom. P.S. call me!" I let out a chuckle and wipe away some tears, realizing how much my mom really knows me, and how much I freaking love her.

I put the food and the water bottle in my backpack and Mom's note in the breast pocket of my flannel shirt, leaving the envelope of twenties untouched. I amble to the front door but stop short and then walk backwards to the kitchen table. On second thought, I could use the extra cash. Besides, I will be paying it all back. I grab a few twenties, stuff them into my back pocket, and head out the front door, closing it as quietly as I can.

*　　*　　*

I'm sitting in the front passenger seat of a van. A woman named Kim is at the wheel, and we're headed west down Highway 5. After leaving Mom's house, I made the two-mile walk to the interstate, where I set up camp with my backpack and guitar case on the side of the road. After about half an hour of sticking my thumb out, Kim picked me up. She is a big woman, in her forties, and she is the type of person who doesn't settle for any nonsense. She asked me where I'm going, and I told her.

After jumping into the passenger seat, Kim accelerates to merge onto the highway, and we're off. Kim asks me, "What's your business in Rockwood?" She glances over at me. "A young girl like you shouldn't be hitching a ride out here, there are a lot of weirdos out there."

"Well," I reply. "Ain't got much, and need everything I have for when I get to Rockwood." This is only partly true. "I've got a friend there. She's a musician and is going to help me find gigs."

"So, you're a musician, too?" asks Kim.

"Well, I hope so. I haven't been playing much lately, but I plan on changing that."

Kim smiles at me, "Well, I wish you the best of luck. The world needs fine music. It's good for the soul."

Kim tells me that she can take me as far as Springfield, but then she will be heading south after that. I figure I can catch another ride from there.

During the next few hours, we chat about the weather, our favorite bands, and other stuff. Kim is friendly, and a widow. She has three kids and drives the van delivering medical supplies to make some extra money.

We soon come to the outskirts of Springfield. I tell Kim that she can drop me at a rest area along the highway.

There are a few cars and semi-trucks parked in the lot, and a family picnicking under a tree. As we pull into a parking spot, Kim turns to me, and her cheery expression disappears.

"Ash, you be very careful around here. I didn't want to tell you at first, but there have been reports of missing girls from these parts. Girls about your age."

I nod my head but think nothing of it. Kim probably means well, trying to scare me into not hitchhiking. I look at her, "I'll be careful, Kim, don't worry about that. I'm a big girl." I try to sound tough and confident, but it just comes out awkward.

Kim leans over and puts her arm on mine. "There's talk of a serial killer on the loose. They call him the 'Monsoon Killer' because he only kills when it rains, or something like that. I'm not kidding. Just take care of yourself and don't get in a car with any weirdos."

I smile at Kim and place my hand on top of hers. "Will do.

Thanks so much for the ride, I really appreciate it."

I open the passenger door, hop down onto the hot pavement, and wave at Kim. She returns it with a smile. Then she drives away, heading south, down the highway to Springfield. Slinging my backpack over my shoulders, I march in the direction of a truck stop just a half-mile away from the rest stop.

*　　*　　*

As trucks, vans, and cars pass by me, I trudge along the shoulder of the highway. It's a beautiful spring day, just a few clouds floating across the azure sky above. I look up, trying to shield the sun from my eyes, and notice a hawk circling above, probably looking for its lunch below. Soon after, I reach the truck stop and decide to get a soda before hitching another ride. I follow a family with two screaming toddlers through the door of the Stop and Shop and make a beeline to the refrigerated sodas. A couple of cowboys look me up and down, I ignore them. Don't feel like making any small talk, just want to get a Coke and hit the road again.

I wait impatiently in line behind a couple of truckers, digging out one of the twenties to pay for the Coke. I can hear one of the toddlers crying as the mother grabs a bag of Cheetos from her hand. I love kids but can't bear the screaming and the crying. I pay up with the cashier, a tall, lanky teenager, and blow out the door.

The truck stop is busy, almost every pump is occupied. On the trucker side of the pumps, there are several semis. I walk over, lugging my guitar case and my Coke in the other hand. There's a group of truckers hanging around talking. Interrupting their conversations, I ask if anyone would be willing to give me a ride to Rockwood, or anyplace west of here. The truckers shake their heads, say that they aren't heading in that direction. I thank them, and then go around to hit up a few other people, one guy with a van, and an older woman driving a truck. Unfortunately for me, they aren't going that way either.

I hang out on the curb next to the sandwich shop. The whiff of smoked meat and melted cheese makes my stomach rumble, and I realize that I haven't eaten since the night before. I sit down on the curb and take out one of Mom's sandwiches. The banana, peanut butter, and jelly brings me back to middle school.

I used to eat my lunch by the running track, where I could watch the other grades practice and compete, since we didn't share the same lunch time. I never liked playing sports myself, but I've always enjoyed watching people run.

I wash down the sandwich with some Coke, and consider having a chocolate-chip cookie, but opt to save it for later. As I take another gulp of Coke, I detect a bizarre sensation. All of a sudden, my body feels shivery. I scan the area. Nothing is out of the ordinary.

Then I notice a man sitting under a tree, across the lot, maybe 200 yards from me. I watch him for a while, hoping my sunglasses won't give away the fact that I'm staring at him. It's bizarre, he has a chessboard and pieces laid out in front of him on the pavement. Seems like he's playing by himself. I drain my Coke and crush the can, considering approaching the guy for a lift. I get on my feet, dust my pants, gather my belongings, and stroll across the parking lot.

As I near him, his concentration on the board doesn't falter. The chess game with the phantom adversary is occupying all his mental capacity. He looks middle-aged, some grey hairs peeping out from under his ball cap. He is wearing a dark, long, hooded jacket. Medium height and build. I stop a few feet from him. He is sitting cross-legged in front of a battered, wooden chessboard.

I shift my feet, then murmur, "Are you…"

The man swiftly and enthusiastically moves a white chess piece across the board. He's still not showing any sign that he is aware of my presence.

I clear my throat, "Excuse…."

The man abruptly puts a finger to his lips, eyes still transfixed on the board. I fidget, wondering what to do next. After a few seconds, he moves a black piece. Then he slowly looks up at me. The moment my eyes meet his gaze it sends chills up my spine. Those icy cold, penetrating orbs of cornflower blue are deceptively calm. Flecks of gold and brown suffuse the dark grey pupils. Transfixed by his devastating eyes, I'm not able to move a muscle. Inexplicably, it feels like I'm staring down into a barrel of a gun instead of a pair of human eyes.

His deep voice breaks the reverie. "Yeah?"

I gulp, "Are you playing chess…against yourself?"

He throws me a quizzical look. "I play only when it's a sure thing." Then he returns his attention back to the chessboard. I scratch my head.

He stares at the board for another minute, then sighs and starts putting away his chess pieces.

"Are you done? It was just getting fun," I tease.

The man gazes at me with those piercing eyes. "No, but you've ruined it."

My face is burning. "Sorry."

He continues to put away the pieces in silence, and I notice that his hands are expressive and seem almost soft, like the fingers of a pianist.

I perceive that this guy is most likely unwilling to give me a ride, assuming he's even going in the same direction. And frankly, I'm not too excited about the prospect of getting one from him either. Although I'm desperate to be on my way and definitely don't want to get stuck at this shoddy truck stop all night, this guy makes the hair on my neck stand on end. Sooner or later, someone else will come along.

I start to turn around when he says, "Sure."

This startles me. "Pardon?"

"I can take you as far as Clinton."

My skin is swathed with goosebumps. Is he a psychic? I turn back. "How'd you…"

"Heard you asking around." He snaps the box closed and stands up. He's a few inches taller than me. His face is cleanly shaven with an angular jawline and a thin-lipped, unsmiling mouth.

"Oh…" I reply. "And while I go around asking everyone, you didn't bother to offer me then?"

He closes the gap between us, and my heart skips a beat.

"Not the volunteering type, but since you interrupted my game—" he explains matter-of-factly.

I roll my eyes, an annoying habit of mine, according to my mother. "I was gonna wait for you to finish the game and ask nicely."

He starts to walk away. Thinking that I had pissed him off, I just stand still, watching his receding back. I'm about to throw in the towel and move on when he speaks, "Come or don't, it's your move." I knit my brows, blown away by the stranger's eccentricity, and contemplating the half-offer. In the end, the urge to get away and the intangible intrigue surrounding the man win the day.

The man walks faster across the parking lot, towards a black truck parked next to a dumpster overflowing with boxes and trash. I rush after him, stumbling a few times, and almost drop my guitar case. I curse to myself and soon catch up with him. He opens the driver's side of his truck and starts the engine. Realizing that an invitation is out of the question, I reach for the passenger door, but it doesn't budge. I give him a look through the window and knock. Without so much as a glance, he unlocks it. I swing open the door and step into the passenger seat, parking my guitar case on my lap. I remove my backpack that is digging into my back and put it close to my feet. I am immediately struck by the pine air freshener. The smell is so strong that it stings my nostrils a little.

The interior of the truck is immaculate; no sign of empty soda cans, fast-food wrappers, or other stuff people usually leave in their cars. Not even a speck of dust on the dashboard, or a particle wedged between the ridges of the floor mat. He pulls out of the parking lot and onto the entrance ramp of the highway.

"Is this a new truck?" I ask. He glances over at me silently. Apparently, he's still in a grouchy mood—more than likely it's a permanent feature, but that doesn't sway me. "It looks new but maybe it's because you take good care of it." I am trying to lighten the mood a bit by complimenting him.

He passes a slow-moving semi, pulls back into the right lane, and then finally answers, "Cleanliness is next to godliness."

"So that means I can't pick my nose in here?" Oh god, I just blurt that out and it sounds so stupid. Sometimes, when I'm nervous, I say dumb stuff.

He replies, "Well, you could. But then I'd have to chop off that finger and force-feed it to ya." There isn't any emotion displayed on his face as he's stating this. Then he adds, "Outside the truck, of course."

I feel a lump form in my throat. Weird sense of humor, but then again, everything about him is. I joke, "Look at Gandhi here. Chill, man. I need all my fingers to play the guitar. If you're going to be that way this is going to be the longest ride of my life." I grip my guitar case tightly and start to regret getting in his truck.

He responds, "Likewise."

An awkward silence ensues. "Can I fart at least?"

*   *   *

A few hours pass, and we drive the speed limit on the interstate, past cornfields, truck stops, farms, and dinky little towns. This part of the country is flat, not a hill or mountain in sight. Watching the stretch of highway before me, I start to get a little drowsy from the monotonous scenery. So I decide to attempt to make conversation again.

"So, what's your name?" I ask.

"Why?"

"Are you for real?" This guy is starting to really get under my skin.

He looks straight ahead, just one hand on the wheel. I've heard about men of few words, but this guy takes the cake.

I push for at least a name, not wanting to call him 'you' the whole time. "So?" I press. He squints. I spell it out for him. "Your n-a-m-e."

"What's in a name?" he grunts. "I tell you and you think you know all about me? Best friends?" I notice that he's gripping the steering wheel so hard, his knuckles turn white. He adds, "Why does it matter?"

"Wow," I say. "Congratulations! You actually manage to speak more than one sentence at a time!" I sneer. "If it doesn't matter, how about I call you Betty Boop, then?" That's a little much, but he is really pissing me off.

He shrugs and shakes his head. "You people are funny," he counters.

"What's that?" That is a weird-ass answer. 'You people?' Is he not of the human race?

"Never mind," he says, easing his death-grip on the steering wheel. We ride in silence for a while more. Then he interjects, "Ty."

"Is that a name?" Not really a question, just want to get some reaction out of this alien. "Or something you like to put on while doing hot yoga?" I mumble the last part under my breath. No response. Not sure if he heard.

"Ok Ty," I give in. "My name is Ash." I extend my hand for a handshake, but he just nods.

I retract my hand and mutter, "Course not. Bacteria and all that good stuff."

More silence as we drive down the interstate. The rumbling of the truck's engine is starting to get on my nerves. We can use some music right about now. So I put one finger on the tuning knob and ask, "Radio? Yeah? Even you like music, right?"

Ty shakes his head.

"Come on! What's your vice? RnB? Jazz? Don't tell me… Country!" Even discussing music with this guy is tons better than the silence. I turn the radio on anyway. Nothing.

"Hate music." He announces it just like telling me that he doesn't take sugar with his coffee, just when I think that things can't get any odder for him. Who hates music, honestly?

I have to ask, "Who in their right mind hates music? Why?" Me, the musician with a guitar in my lap.

He replies, "Noises. All the time."

"Really? Right now? Where? I don't hear anything."

He taps the side of his head.

Curious, I keep on. "Yeah? What kind of noise?"

Then, suddenly, he throws his head back and screeches. A blood-curdling, bone-chilling howl that just about deals me a heart attack. The thought of being trapped in a cell of an insane asylum with a nutcase crosses my mind. Another lump takes shape, clogging my esophagus. This is getting too kooky for my liking.

But I'm not about to let him scare me, so I comment calmly, despite my quickening heartbeat, "What the hell was that? Were you going for heavy metal? Sounds more like a petrified pig with a half-slit throat."

Ty keeps quiet, looking straight ahead at the road, like nothing happened.

I should but don't feel like letting things go so easily. "Do you hate puppies and ice cream too?"

He glances over his shoulder, face as serious as a pandemic, "Yes."

*   *   *

After hearing his latest confession, I figure it's time to give our conversation a rest. Enough negativity for a whole week. We ride on. The more we stay silent, the heavier the air feels. Like a darkening cloud, pregnant with moisture. Finally, Ty pulls into a truck stop. There are a few cars and semis, a large family with six kids, and a little dog wandering around one of the pumps. I must use the toilet, but I'm unsure about leaving my guitar with Ty. But he did say that he hates music. And that hopefully would make him think twice about bailing and leaving me high and dry at the truck stop, should that cross his mind. It's silly, I know, but that thought gives me a little peace of mind. Despite his antics, Ty is alright, I guess. Wouldn't want to try my luck again to find another ride in these hours.

Furthermore, we're not that far now from Rockwood. Can almost see it in my mind's eye; a charming, lively city by the lake. I have been there once, visiting Lauren.

We get out and he starts pumping gas. I ask him if he wants anything from the shoppette. As usual, he just stares at me. I offer him a twenty for gas, but he shakes his head and looks away. Can't say I didn't try. After using the ladies' room, I pick up a bottle of water and a bag of chips for later.

As I follow the huge family out to the pumps, I find that Ty and the truck are gone. I shake my head, kicking myself for being so stupid. He's a creep and is probably happy to be rid of me. I look up at the sky, soaking in the sun, the smells of diesel and fried food permeating my nostrils. There's a honk coming from behind me. I turn. It's Ty in the truck; he didn't ditch me after all. Feeling both relieved and a tiny bit anxious, I walk over to where the truck is, next to a tanker, and get in the passenger side.

My guitar is still in the front. Ty has his jacket unzipped; he's wearing a black raincoat underneath. It's peculiar, given the dry and somewhat warm weather. I take a peek at him. How on earth is he not drenched in sweat, having those clothes blanketing his body all this time? Without any warning, his head swivels in my direction. Taken aback, I grin and point at his jacket. "Don't you feel a bit warm in those?"

"No. Never know." That's a very unclear answer but I'm used to Ty's vagueness by now.

We pull out of the truck stop and head back on the highway. The sun is starting to dip beyond the clouds. I wonder how much longer it will be to get to Rockford. According to my phone, we have only about 150 miles to go.

We ride in silence; I have given up hope in attempting to get Ty to converse with me. My eyes start to feel heavy and I'm very close to dozing off.

"Why are you doing this?" he blurts out. I jolt, yanked from fatigue.

"What? Doing what?" I rub my eyes. "Hitching a ride? In a truck with a creep?" Can't help expressing that last part.

My lousy remark doesn't seem to faze him. "Yeah," he speaks casually. "Aren't you worried?"

"Of what?" I massage my temples, trying to wake myself up.

Ty shrugs. Not sure what's up with this guy. Even when he wants to find out about something, he refuses to talk too much. It's like each word pains him, draining his life force or something. So I help him out, "Of being alone with a stranger, miles away from civilization?"

He nods. I challenge, "What's the worst that can happen?

Being robbed?" I gesture at the backpack and the guitar case, my meager possessions. "I got nothing anyway. Raped? My own boyfriend, ex now, can't even stand to look at me." Then I state further for drama, "Serial killer?"

Ty turns his head, biting on his lip. I shake my head and laugh, "What are the chances of that? I'm more likely to win a lottery *and* get struck by lightning than run into a serial killer." Ty breaks the silence with a little chuckle. That shocks me a little.

"This could be your day." He has a leer on his face that makes my skin crawl. Not sure where this conversation is going.

"Not happening unless you're one," I reply.

"Maybe I am," he whispers.

"Come on. If you were, you wouldn't be very good at it. I mean, you're odd as they come, I'll give you that. But what kind of a serial killer is afraid of a little dust?" I goad. "And you don't look like one."

Ty snorts, "What do they look like anyways? If I was one, you should be worried about what I'm not afraid of." The conversation has taken an unexpected turn.

"OK, I'll play along," Ty can be a little fun after all. "If you were a serial killer, then why me? And how do you pick your victim? Or am I your good deed of the week? But like I said, I've got nothing to offer."

"You'd be surprised," he answers. "And, you approached me, remember?"

He has a point. "You are right about that," I admit. "But you only want them to think that way—"

I consider this, then continue, "You let them choose you so that they have their guard down. Right? That's how you hooked me, ain't it?"

"A magician never reveals," he's still grinning. I squint while chewing my lower lip. A moment later, I slap my thigh, exclaiming, "The chessboard! Of course! All you need to do is park yourself in some girl's line of sight, but not too close. Sooner or later, you get their attention. When everyone else at the truck stop is ogling her body up and down, you make it seem like the only thing that you're interested in is the chess game."

I pause to see his reaction, which is his usual stone-faced expression. He continues to drive, concentrating on the road ahead of him. I go on with my theory. "Well, that'd certainly give off an illusion of harmlessness to an innocent, unknowing prey!"

No comment. "I'll admit, that is brilliant, and subtle too. Works every time, does it?"

He mutters, "You're in my truck, aren't you?"

"Touché," I concede. "What you gonna do with me then? Drag me to your lair in a deserted farmhouse? Chop my body to pieces and put them in jars?"

"Not quite," he refutes. "You watch too much TV."

"Speaking of TV, there were reports of missing girls. You heard of this 'Monsoon Killer'? Kind of a dramatic nickname. He goes into action only when it rains, apparently."

I look out the window. The sun has almost disappeared behind a bank of grey clouds. A pungent, earthy smell enters my nostrils. Out of nowhere, the weather has changed. "Looks like rain is on the way. Watch out, girls!" I jest.

Ty is silent as usual, but he observes the gathering grey clouds with intent.

All this time, I've failed to notice that the chess box is

perched next to Ty, until he picks it up and motions for me to stow it in the glove box.

"Man, you sure are attached to this thing. You sleep with it too?" I take it from him and open the glove box.

My heart lurches. In the glove box is a small leather purse and a pair of pink sunglasses. Unless Ty has an interesting hobby, these items have no business being here. There are also a pair of used white latex gloves. They have been turned inside out, mottled with dry brown stains on the reverse side.

I swallow hard as a freight train of thoughts and questions storms through my head. Whose are those? Why are they there? And what were the gloves used for? The brown specks, are they what I think? I attempt to convince myself that Ty likely has staged it all just to scare me. Some kind of a sick, elaborate joke. He probably does this to all the hitchhikers that come his way.

Another disturbing theory comes to mind. Does Dex have anything to do with this? I wouldn't put it past him. But then, he's never been that smart; this is beyond him. Unavoidably, a far more macabre hunch ignites within.

My hands are a little unsteady. I quickly hide them in my jacket pockets, hoping he didn't see. Could he be—?

Ty is staring at the highway in front of us. But his head is cocked, body rigid, like he's anticipating something. I have to think hard, and fast. Is the son of a bitch trying to tell me something? More likely this is some form of a twisted test. He's trying to rattle me and see my reaction. I shift in my seat. My throat feels dry. "This s'pose to scare me?" I force myself not to take my eyes off him. I swallow hard, hoping he won't see through my tough-girl act.

Ty shrugs. "Don't know what you mean." He's lying. There's a veiled exhilaration in his voice.

I shove the chess box into the glove compartment and slam it shut.

"I usually get more of a reaction than that." He cracks a simper. "Most girls just scream their head off, and then I have to shut them up."

At this point, I figure that Ty, or whoever this lunatic is, is either full of shit, delusional, or that he really is a cold-blooded criminal. Whatever the truth is, despite the bitter taste in the back of mouth, my instinct is screaming at me to seem unafraid and intrigued.

"So, what do you do with them?" I pretend to probe, dreading to hear his response.

"The brides, you mean?" His eyes are still on the road.

"If that's what you call them. Yeah, the brides..." Now my throat is on fire. I'm dying to slake my thirst with some water, but I dare not move. Now for the push. "Are you…him? Did you kill them?" I wrap my fingers around my knife.

"Who says I kill them? They're immortalized. In here." He taps the side of his forehead a couple of times with two fingers. "Not one to kiss and tell."

I desperately want to scream and get him to stop the truck. Fighting the urge to look away, I keep my gaze on him. It's obvious that he's into mind games, so maybe I could fight fire with fire. Think!

"Maybe you're a bride." I turn the tables, my Hail Mary. Every muscle in my body is ready to spring. I wait.

"Don't follow," he squints and looks sideways at me. I have

caught him off guard.

I sigh, as if dealing with an uncomprehending child. "When a lone wolf is in the wilderness too long, it ceases to recognize its own. All it sees is sheep." I'm hoping this will disorient him.

He's quiet and motionless for several seconds. Then it sinks in. "No…" he mutters under his breath. Then he hits the brakes hard. We screech to a halt on the asphalt. I almost hit my head against the dashboard. Fortunately, ours is the only vehicle on the road.

"No way!" he hisses. He doesn't even bother to pull the truck to the side of the road. The engine is left running.

"That's right, I picked you."

The look on his face as he analyzes me is inhospitable and fervent. "You are the bride, and I'm the lone wolf."

I pretend that our unscheduled stop doesn't faze me. "Not my job to convince you."

Ty's eyes narrow and he leans towards me. We lock eyes. Those piercing eyes are slowly sucking the life right out of me. I know then that it's crucial for me to get out of this truck and away from this monster.

"Uh, I need to pee," I announce. That was a mistake.

Ty smirks, "So you can run away and get help?"

Playing the tough girl, I answer, "I can handle you fine by myself."

"Yeah? Show me what you got, Ash." The way he says my name makes my insides cringe.

Before I know it, he has my left wrist and is twisting it backward. Despite his delicate-looking hands, his grip is solid and full of force. With his other hand, he yanks my shirt, shoving me forward against the dashboard. Then he slithers closer.

His face is just inches from mine. His breath smells of

strong mint. But there is a slight underlying odor of a decay, like rotting fish.

He seizes a bunch of hair on the back of my head and veers my head so we're face-to-face. A sneer smears his visage. It disappears as soon as he realizes that an object is being held to his neck, its point pressing just below the ear.

"A slasher, huh? Should've known," he mumbles.

He winks as I prop the knife firmly onto his throat. "Not fooling anyone, little girl. Think you got the pluck to plunge that into someone? Or is it just for cutting apples?"

I'm so close to breaking. I exert more pressure on the knife, the sharp blade draws a trickle of blood from the clean-shaven skin.

"One way to find out," I warn as menacingly as I can, waiting for him to make a move. My heart is beating at an alarming speed.

His Medusa-like glower is seconds away from taking away my nerve. I reach down deep into my soul, barely clinging to the belief that this precise moment determines my fate. After what seems like two lifetimes, he loosens his grip from the back of my hair. Without a word, he shifts the gear into drive and keeps going.

I hesitantly lower my knife, half expecting him to jump me again. He takes out a handkerchief from his breast pocket and wipes the blood from the side of his neck. He moans with disgust. "Look what you did, this is my good one, too!" He rolls the window down and throws the soiled handkerchief out into the wind. Then he rolls up the window.

"Don't you fucking do that again. I'll cut you up so fast and watch you bleed like a stuck pig." I'm trying to sound like I mean it while gingerly putting away my knife.

Ty cackled. "You wouldn't hurt a fly."

"You're right, I wouldn't. Flies don't fight back; they don't beg for mercy and try to outsmart you at the same time. Where's the fun in that?" I must continue the illusion that I'm not just another pawn in his stupid game.

He looks at me over his shoulder. "This is all merely empty words."

"I don't see you walking the walk either. A pair of gloves dotted with ketchup doesn't exactly make me tremble with fear!" I take a gulp of water, hoping the cool liquid will prevent my voice from cracking.

We ride on in silence for a few more miles, until we get to another truck stop. I really need the toilet this time, a wave of nausea sweeps over me.

I get out before the engine dies. I can feel Ty's eyes boring a hole in my back as I stride in the direction of the gas station.

*   *   *

I stumble into an older lady with purple hair and a Hawaiian shirt coming out of the women's room. I mutter an apology and make my way to the sink. After turning on the faucet, I splash my face with cold water. A mom and two girls are also in the restroom. One of the little girls is crying, while the tired-looking mother tries in vain to comfort her. They both look as exhausted as I feel.

While attempting to bring back some life with the cool running water, I drag my hands down my cheeks and catch a glimpse of myself in the mirror. I look like crap, pale and solemn as Wednesday Addams, shadowy circles under the eyes and hunched shoulders. The shaking of my hands is worsening.

I had startled myself by pulling a knife on that psycho; no doubt I was playing with fire. Haven't got a clue what he's done or what he's capable of. Frankly, it's better to keep things that way. But it's imperative for me to know him a little and to sort of anticipate what he'd do next. I must keep up the pretense and at the same time make it somewhat plausible to him. It's impossible to get any reading from the unpredictable and cryptic Ty.

I pull down a couple of paper towels from the steel dispenser and dry my face and hands. I examine my face again in the mirror and shake my head, cursing my luck for crossing paths with Ty. The mom and two kids finally leave, and I'm the only one in the restroom. Then an idea strikes me.

I hurriedly lock the door to the women's room, move the tall garbage can, turn it upside down, and place it under a solitary window. Going back in the truck with that psycho is insufferable, the idea of slipping out the window and running away is a no-brainer. I climb up on the trash can and unlatch the rusted window, but something in the back of my mind stops me. What if he's expecting this? He would've easily seen through this. As I stand on the garbage can in limbo, I wonder if he's just outside the window? Anticipating that I'll play straight into his hands. Upon further deliberation, I abort the plan, hopping down from the trash can.

The lure of an instant escape from the madman was almost too irresistible. Finding myself yet again behind the sink, I wonder as to what my next steps should be. My knife will not protect me from him for much longer. It's going to take a lot more than just sharp metal and wit to stave off those black-hole eyes.

Someone knocks on the door of the restroom. I stay still. My hands are gripping the sides of the porcelain sink, body slightly stooped forward, every muscle taut with tension. I close my eyes and take deep long breaths. Reopening my eyes, I feel slightly improved.

With no hesitation, I slap myself hard on the cheek. Before regaining my composure, I give the other side of my face the same wonderful treatment. My ears are ringing. The knock on the door becomes banging. After taking another brief assessment of myself in the mirror, I walk over to unlock the door.

There's a young woman with a toddler. She reads me the riot act for locking the door and then rushes to one of the stalls. Without apologizing, I just leave. Walking out the double doors of the truck stop, I brace myself for the mayhem ahead.

*　　*　　*

The truck is gone. My heart skips a beat. Do I dare believe that he really left? Perhaps he lost interest in me. Or maybe he found a juicier target. No Ash, that is so wrong. I wouldn't put my worst enemy in a truck with that psycho. I feel my throat close, hoping against hope that I've seen the last of him.

As I round the corner of the building, I almost walk right into Ty. "Going somewhere?" he inquires.

My heart sinks, I try to keep my face straight. "Looking for you. Thought you bailed, mighta bored you to death."

He sneers. "You? Not a chance."

"Good! Wouldn't want to lose my ride." I lie freely through my teeth.

As casually as possible, I scan the truck stop. For about two seconds, I consider just breaking free and screaming for help.

But then my eyes catch his hand slithering inside his coat pocket. Looks like he's holding something. A gun? My thoughts turn to the woman with a young child, in the washroom. Things can get ugly real quick if I were to force his hands. That may easily turn the whole thing into a hostage situation. Or a small massacre. Ty signals for me to walk ahead of him.

The truck is parked out back, facing the building, less than twenty feet away from my escape-route window of the washroom.

Without uttering a word, I get in the truck. Ty puts the keys in the ignition, starts it up, and pulls out of the truck stop.

Ty takes something out of his pocket, and I freeze. As he pulls his hand from the pocket, I breathe a silent sigh of relief. It's a chocolate bar. I look in the rearview mirror at the truck stop. Only now I feel a pang of dismay. Had I known that it wasn't a gun in his pocket, I could have ended things back then and there. My best chance of escaping has vanished, my hopes of getting out of this alive are quickly dissipating.

*   *   *

We are on the road again. I notice that Ty is kind of fidgety. He keeps shifting his position in the driver's seat, scratching the back of his neck, and drumming his fingers on the steering wheel. Inside my jacket pocket, I place one hand on the knife, in case he tries to jump me again. His restlessness is making me nervous as a cat. While I'm taking a sip from my water bottle, unexpectedly, Ty breaks the deafening silence.

"Tell me more about your conquests." I almost choke on my water. The hairs on my neck stand on end.

I clear my throat and keep my hand on the knife. "Well, I'm not one to kiss and tell either." I stay my ground, trying to keep up the black widow act, hoping it will buy me some more time.

"Fair," he nods. "How about just a little peek? Do you exclusively go after men?" He's rubbing his neck where I held the blade. It's red and probably irritating.

"Yeah." I take another gulp of water.

"How many men have you killed?" He sure is getting chatty now.

"Enough." And I've become as taciturn as he is, not wanting to give him too much and trip up. Just enough to keep him sated. "I think I've had enough of this bullshit. How about some quiet?" I try to deflect.

"How come there isn't tons of reports of missing men?" Ty probes.

I must think of something fast. My life may be dependent on my answers. No pressure, Ash. "The general public and the news treat men differently from women, you know that." I pray to whoever is up there that he'll buy this home-brewed, out-of-my-ass theory. "And who says I'm from around here? I could've operated anywhere. The world is there for the taking."

Operate is probably not the best choice of words in the serial-killing business. But hey, I was going for subtle.

"Okay. Go on." A few raindrops hit the windshield, and I hope to hell it won't start pelting down.

I continue. "When men don't turn up, everyone assumes that they skip town, have an affair, shirk their manly responsibilities, like running away from debt, and so on. On the other hand, when women go missing, the first thing in everybody's mind is that they've been hurt. That's why news of missing men doesn't generate the same level of anxiety and interests as their counterparts." Did that sound lame? My throat is parched, so I drink some more water and bounce in the passenger seat as we drive over a pothole.

"Bottom line, the disappearances of men don't sell news. That, combined with the general public misconception of male immunity, works wonders. That makes the hunt for the homeless, people with no close family, unsavory characters with dubious records as convenient as picking lettuce from a grocery store. Either no one will miss them or they're expected to disappear by their own free will, sooner or later."

I pause for effect and add, "You said you have no one. You'd be a prime candidate." I take a stab at imitating one of his soulless smiles, not sure if it comes out as intended. At the same time, my pulse is beating hard in my ears.

"I did say that, didn't I?" admits Ty.

"Besides," I press, keep striking while the iron is hot. "Even though you don't look homeless, you do fit the unsavory character part." I'm not sure how long I can retain this cat-and-mouse.

"Uh-oh, someone's in trouble!" I note a tone of mockery and doubt in his voice. My hands start to sweat, and my heart skips a beat. Ty is relentlessly scrutinizing me to find an opening, waiting for a wrong move.

"Get off your fucking high horse and start treating me with some respect. Because I deserve it, and you're no better than me." I snap. "Or just shut the fuck up, get me to Clinton and we've never met." Please, please don't let him lose it. I hold my breath.

"Ok, how about I show you mine and you show me yours? Just a little game to pass the time?" He's far from done, completely ignoring what I just stated. Now the game is taking another menacing turn.

"You realize that we aren't exactly two BFFs exchanging vacation stories, right?"

He shrugs. "Same difference. You go first."

The most excruciating part about this ordeal is the not knowing. First and foremost, if he's really who he claims he is. If he is, I wonder whether he's made up his mind about me or not. If he's toying with me. Or if he's treating this as an audition, to determine if I'm like him, if I should live to see tomorrow. "I'd like to make my victims suffer," I respond.

"No, no, no," Ty interrupts. "Any teenager who's seen an episode of CSI knows that. I want personal, juicy details."

I'm so exhausted I could sleep for one week straight. A weird thought comes to my mind; this must be what speed dating for serial killers is like, if there ever was one. "OK," I say, "I'd let a scumbag in a dark hat and coat pick me up, then I'd toy with him a little. I'd lure him to a quiet place, maybe offer him a bit of fun, and then when the moment is right, I'd cut his throat from ear to ear, and watch the life flow out of his body."

"Textbook answer. But what if your victim isn't interested in a 'bit of fun?' How would you lure him then?" He is really enjoying this.

"Fuck you and your little game." I'm getting pissed and frightened. This is getting out of hand. "I'll write a book about my 'conquests,' publish it so you can read all about it. How about that? Maybe I'll dedicate it to you so we can exchange letters from the comfort of our own supermax facilities."

Ty's jaw tightens, and he grips the steering wheel hard, baring those white knuckles. I bet he's not used to getting sassed. By a woman too. I'm walking on eggshells.

"Your turn. Ask me. You don't like it then, we stop." He slowly loosens his grip on the wheel. That was a close one, a bullet dodged.

That sounded like an order. I don't have much choice. I turn to him and sigh deeply. "Are all your hypothetical victims hitchhikers?"

"That's weak, Ash." He tsk-tsks me. "No."

"You need to give me more details than that," I argue.

"Nope," he says. "That's strike one."

"Who made you judge?"

"Me. My turn. Are your hypothetical victims an embodiment of someone from your past?" He flashes a wolf-like grin.

That takes me by surprise, what is he getting at? I answer, "Maybe."

"Daddy's a baddie?"

Ty must think he's Hannibal Lecter. I keep quiet.

"Struck a chord, huh?" he nods to himself. "You're an open book, Ash." He pronounces my name like he's dragging it over hot gravel. I wince.

Time to make another move. "How do you feel about the rain, Ty?" This is risky, but I need to keep control of the flow of the conversation.

His eyes narrow, a brilliant spark ignites in those arcs of gloom. After several seconds of silence, he speaks. "Have you ever noticed how people react to an unscheduled event of a downpour? Everyone scrambles for cover, even animals. Cars honking left and right. Suddenly everybody has the need to get to a safe place, away from the rain, as if they were droplets of toxic liquid. One second everything's normal and in the next, mayhem and chaos sweep over, leaving behind scattered litter, empty streets, and silence. What an imposing force!"

I'm amazed by this speech of his. I don't think he's ever talked this much at once with his own mother. He prattles on. "Always loved the rain. Embodies some sort of a rebirth, a cleansing. It's like a restart button for your soul, all this accumulated murk that's clouding your thoughts, feelings, potentials. Everything is wiped off and you get a clean slate. And then comes this indefatigable itch to express yourself. To be free, to finally be able to break out those repressed desires. Y'know?"

I don't.

*   *   *

We drive on in silence. The rain abates. The moon and the stars emerge, glittering in the cloudless, ethereal sky. I'd like to think this is a good omen, that maybe the universe is telling me something.

Then my thoughts drift back to my mom, and the night she did a reading. She couldn't or didn't want to tell me what she saw that frightened her. Why didn't she stop me? It was probably very vague. She wouldn't know what it was exactly, the when and the how. I think all she saw was an unexplainable darkness. What was she supposed to say? All she could do was warn me, which she did.

Ty languidly pulls onto the off-ramp of the highway, makes a right turn at a battered old stop sign, and parks on the side of the road. We aren't very far from the highway, but he is careful to pull near a copse of trees, just out of view. If anything happens here, none of the drivers on the highway would see it. Screaming wouldn't do any good either, having to compete with the roar of highway traffic.

So much for a good omen.

Is this it? Is that all there is?

Didn't get to say goodbye to Mom, not really. I touch the front pocket where her letter is kept. I can feel the crinkling of paper under the slight pressure of my fingertips.

Time for last tango.

I unlatch my case, open it, and deliberately take out my rosewood parlor guitar. She feels cold to the touch. She senses and mimics my feelings. In a lot of ways, she's been my soulmate throughout the years.

Through thin and thick, she's always been there for me. To cry with me, to lift me up, to help me find my inner peace and strength.

I put her on my lap and start caressing her soothingly. Fingers tracing the ridges of her neck and body, a muted sigh escapes my lips. I know these nooks and curves like the back of my own hand.

"Please tell me you're not playing that." Ty looks alarmed. Ignoring him, I fingerpick a tune. The rich, sparkly tone awakens something in me. The rhythm of my plucking is becoming more fluid as I begin to play an acoustic number. It's a piece that I know by heart that has become a vital part of me, a ballad that defines who I was and am.

Ty is silent. I play on. The sorrow of the melody compels me to reminisce. Snapshots and reels from my past flood my mind. Can't help but be overwhelmed and get carried away by these floating, colliding memories from the deep recesses of my brain.

"Hmm..." Ty mumbles as I finish.

"Hmm what?" I pray he doesn't notice the slight tremble in

my voice. My mask of bravado is cracking. Soon he will only see an insignificant, petrified prey.

"Sufferable." His eyes are trained on mine. "Song means something to you?"

"Yes." I'm going for broke. "In fact, you'll be the first and only person to be alive after hearing me play it."

"How's that?"

"Use your imagination."

"Is that what you do when you realize they have nothing left to offer? One last squeeze before you throw out the peel?"

That's distressingly disturbing. I shrug.

His eyes widen and he leans forward a little. "Tell me."

"You know what, it's none of your bloody business. I'm done with this summer-camp story-swapping nonsense."

His face becomes taut. A vein bulges on his neck. His glare is like a scalpel dissecting my every cell that's just barely holding my body together. I brace myself for the worst. Just when I'm about to disintegrate and plead for mercy, he breaks off the staring contest.

He takes out a ciggy and a lighter from his front pocket. After lighting the cigarette, he promptly takes a long drag. The glowing ember from the tip hovers like a firefly in the night sky.

"Didn't think you smoke."

He blows out a fat ring of smoke, which glides above my head and disappears into the overhead.

"Saved it for a special occasion?"

He tilts his head back and settles it on the headrest. "My thing with the brides is connection."

"Sex?"

Scowling, he crinkles his nose. "Filthy! I'm talking about a much more sophisticated and profound kind of metaphysical union." He takes another long drag and exhales.

"After a while, the struggle, the torturing, the crying are no longer as gratifying. The real fun begins close to the end. When they're done with all the praying and the begging, ultimately having lost all hope. It's astonishing to witness the flame in one's eyes gradually dwindle and then eventually turn to ash.

"By then, it finally dawns on them that they're damaged beyond repair. And that the only thing in the world that matters, that they lust after, is death. Because it's the only way. To stop the pain, the humiliation, and the agony.

"At that exact moment, an unbreakable bond between us is forged. It's more potent than love, sex, or anything I've experienced."

The sick fuck. My head feels like it's about to implode. A very strong urge to purge the content of my stomach overwhelms my very being. Panicking, I pinch my right thigh as hard as I could.

"Specialists like us don't have the luxury to attend conferences to discuss our craft with one another. If we're really alike, enlighten me." He pauses, watching my reaction. "Why is playing the song such an important aspect of your ritual?"

Specialist? Did he just fucking call himself that?

I shake my head. "Fine, if you must know. You guessed earlier that my brides personify a familiar figure from my past. Well, that has something to do with the song. Happy?"

"I already knew that. What's the connection?" He's practically salivating.

Throwing my hands up in the air, I exhale noisily. "You're a goddamn cactus in my butt!" That doesn't seem to dissuade him.

I begin with a sigh as deep as the Mariana Trench.

"There was this man who lived in our trailer, on and off. Mom fell head over heels for him. She always had a knack for finding good-for-nothing guys to date. We didn't know it at the time but he's the absolute worst of the bunch.

"He was paying me some attention but not overtly. However, his ways of showing affection to me quickly escalated. Soon enough, he'd be asking me to rub his back, giving me pocket money, making borderline inappropriate comments on my clothes and body parts. Should've known he was up to something but honestly, I was just happy for Mom to have someone who treated her decently, without raising a hand or hooking her up with drugs.

"He did all this in the presence of my mom. But she turned a blind eye, not wanting to believe her gut instinct."

I pause and take a big gulp of water. It's becoming unbearably hot in the truck. A little suffocating as well. Beads of sweat line my forehead, just under my fringe. My t-shirt is plastered to my back. I lower the window on my side. He's still working on his ciggy. The heat doesn't seem to bother him one bit.

"One day, I was left alone with him. He came to my room with a bottle of beer in his hand. He was all friendly and chatty. He sat on the edge of my bed and offered me beer. I was a teenager and a drink offer from an adult was like a free ticket to a rock concert, so I took it. While I was sipping beer, his hand wandered onto my thigh. Slapping his hand away, I shot him a dirty look. Not backing down, he told me how beautiful I was, how he'd been dying to make me feel special. He even tried to kiss me. Realizing that he wasn't gonna stop, I screamed at him, threatening to tell Mom and call the cops. His face got all twisted; that charming face instantly turned beastly.

"He called me a tease, among others, for taking his money and beer but refusing his advances. I asked if he cared about Mom at all. Said that he was doing her a favor for trying to groom the bitch of a daughter into a woman. When I threatened to tell Mom again, he welcomed it. He swore that he was gonna leave Mom and tell her that I had attempted to seduce him several times and he'd had enough, promising that Mom would never forgive me for the act of betrayal.

"Mom was so blindly in love that I actually believed him—that Mom would take his side and disown me, if it came to that.

"He stomped out of the room while swearing, banging things. Reluctantly, I followed him into the bedroom.

"His gym bag was open, lying on the bed. He was starting to throw his stuff into the bag. I begged him to stay. Ignoring me, he kept on packing. Then I cried. Told him that I was sorry. He stopped and asked how sorry. Wasn't sure how to respond to that. Flashing me a wolfish grin, he walked to a small table beside the mahogany dresser. He began to play his record player. It had a discolored base and a rusty tone arm. It was the same song that he always played when he was screwing Mom. He closed his eyes and ordered me to close the door."

"Let me guess, the same song you played?" Excitement is written all over his face.

I smile weakly. "One day Mom came home earlier from her shift and caught us in the bedroom. She started shrieking and throwing whatever she could grab at him. He was trying to put the blame on me, the slut. But Mom was having none of it. Without the slightest hesitation, she dialed the cops while continuing to hit him with an umbrella. Given no chance to put on his clothes, let alone to gather his things, he stumbled out of the trailer and drove away in a big hurry.

"As if in trance, without looking or speaking to me, Mom built a fire in a pit just outside our trailer. She went back inside and began to drag his belongings outside. I didn't know what to do. I just watched her instead of helping.

"After several trips, she pranced out to the pit, carrying his precious record player, and hurled it into the fire. I picked up a pair of boots and flung them to the blaze. We took turns tossing his things, like two moths flying and dancing dangerously close to the flame. When it was all gone, Mom hugged me, not taking her eyes from the pyre, crying silently."

There are loud, angry honks coming from the highway. Ty is no longer looking at me. He's gazing dreamily at the distant horizon. "Go on."

"We reported him to the police and moved to another park and town. Thought we'd seen the last of him.

"A few months later, he somehow found us. Him and his two buddies, Rick and Ethan, waited for me outside my workplace. They must have known I was on closing duties, by myself. Ambushed me in the parking lot. Threw me onto the back of his pickup truck.

"There was no music that night. But my mind began to play the same damn song that I'd grown to loathe. Playing it over and over in my head, like a broken record. But it was a different voice. It was my own."

Ty has not moved his cigarette since his last drag. "Under the pale moonlight, the men pinning me down and holding a knife to my face, they took their turn. The bastard, his two cronies, and a beer bottle."

Ty is still. Can't see his face but his neck and shoulders seem tense. "What happened to him?"

"Don't know. Never saw or heard from again. His face and voice are just blurred memories now. Won't even recognize him if he asks me for directions on the street. The mind is a peculiar thing." I sigh again. "That is why, every time I take someone, I play it. Praying to capture something in their eyes. The only way for me to know if it's him."

Ty takes another puff. "I think you have his forehead," I say. He stops his hand mid-air and turns his head. "Unfortunately, I didn't see the spark of recognition I've been seeking in your eyes."

He resumes to put the cigarette on his lips. "Fortunately for me," he mumbles through his half-open mouth.

"Unless you're a very good actor."

"Not my job to convince you." Taking one last deep drag, he scrolls down his window while exhaling. He takes his left hand off the steering wheel and spreads it open.

There's a sooty, disfigured scar around the center of his left palm. A superficial, unsightly scab of scorched, dead tissues. The mottled surface looks parched and ragged as withered avocado skin.

He twirls the cigarette butt on his right fingers and stubs it out on his deformed palm. There's a subdued hissing sound. I cringe. His expression is that of a seasoned poker player eyeing the most boring hand he's ever dealt with.

He flicks the crushed stub into the darkness.

"Get out," he spouts.

"What?" Didn't see this coming.

Eyes facing forward, he unlocks the doors of the truck. "What about Clinton? You're supposed to get me there!"

"Your problem. Wasted enough of my time."

Too good to be true. A ruse? I'm so giddy with anticipation, might just pass out any second. "You can't just leave me here, in the middle of nowhere!"

"Now! Before I change my mind." His tone is absolute. My heart is exploding with unbound joy.

I grab my guitar case and backpack and let myself out. I slam the door shut and glance at the enigmatic stranger behind the wheel. His visage remains deceptively and dubiously expressionless.

I start to lumber away from the truck, forcing myself to put one foot in front of the other. My heart is pounding like a war drum in my chest.

I'm expecting and waiting for an indication of a U-turn. The opening of his door, a gunshot, or his hands around my neck.

I so badly want to run. It takes everything I have not to. I straighten my shoulders and try to keep my body from shaking.

Then it comes. The swing of the door. Boots crunching against gravel. Light footsteps. Then silence.

Slowly, I turn around.

He throws something to me. Reflexively, I catch it. It's my wallet. Must've pickpocketed it when we tangled.

"Don't try anything I wouldn't do," Ty warns. Mom's address is still listed on my ID.

I impart him a look of hatred and of disdain that would make a child cry, I think.

He casually returns to his car. Without looking back.

I pocket the wallet, turn away, and keep walking. To nowhere.

As long as it's away from *him*.

The truck jolts to life. The wheels move across the gravel. This must be it; I think to myself. He's going to run me over.

Resisting the powerful urge to turn around, I keep my eyes straight ahead, staring at the worn asphalt of a country road.

The rumble of the truck lingers.

Feels like my heart just stops. And the time, too.

My whole body aches. Every joint and muscle is screaming in protest, despairing to just give up and collapse.

My steps become heavier as I trudge on. Every motion is a massive effort. Head starts to throb. Sick to the stomach.

The truck's engine fades to a distant hum until only the sounds of highway traffic remain. Slowing my steps, and with what will left, I turn my head. Nothing. No truck in sight. No Ty.

The chirping of crickets fills the windless night air. Sunburnt grass and reeds carpet the otherwise dry earth on the sides of the road. Outlines of jagged peaks and rolling hills furnish the gloomy horizon.

Tears burst out, flowing, blurring my vision. What little strength I have left seeps out of me. My body turns to jelly. Dropping my guitar case, I fall to my knees, hitting the ragged asphalt. I cover my face with my unsteady hands. Body wracked with sobs, I release an anguished wail.

The distant rumbling of traffic stifles my whimpering. But not the flooding of adrenaline. Nor the torment I feel inside.

Towering shadows of enormous, warped willow trees crisscross the bleak terrain around me.

The sickle-shaped moon looms indifferently, basking in its russet, harsh glow.

From somewhere nearby, a hoot of an owl arises. Its day has just begun.

It sounds famished. Time to roam and lie in wait. For an unsuspecting mark.

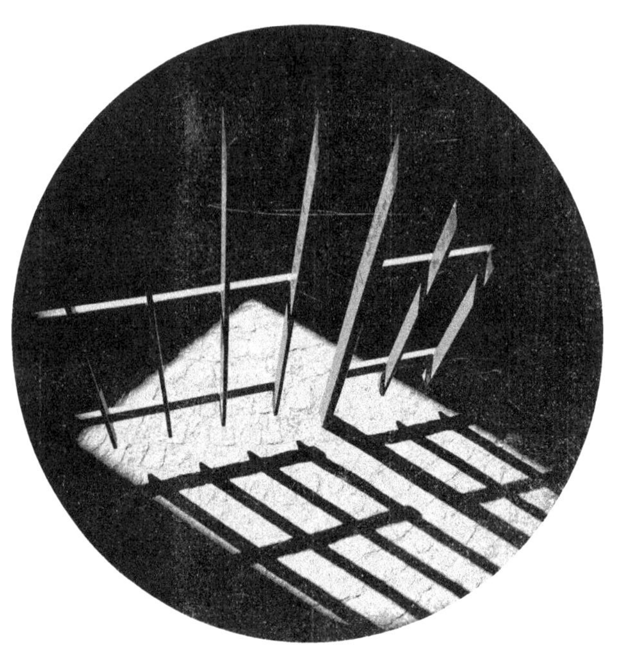

ALL DAY AND A NIGHT

A grey brume drifted slowly across icy black water, like a ghostly spectre. It obscured an islet that was waiting in the distance. At the end of a creaky wooden dock jutting out of Collins Bay, two men stood solemnly, staring out into the silver murk. The dock held the men in its sway as the brume skated onward, the two figures captive as if taken hostage. Pale morning light bled from behind a tree-lined horizon and a soft ashen luster possessed the two spectators like it contained some center.

The first man, Peter, sniffed his runny nose and pulled back the sleeve of his parka to check his watch before glancing out over the bay again.

"Surprised the lake hasn't froze over," he said.

"Owner says it rarely does before midwinter," his companion, Matthew, responded. "Water's so deep."

The two men were dressed similarly in their thermal snow-camo parkas and slacks with waterproof sheepskin boots, thick woolen toques and insulated leather gloves. Each had a soft rifle case and overnight duffel bag at his feet.

"You sure he's coming?" asked Peter.

"Six in the a.m." Matthew's expression was calm. "North

side landing."

"Maybe we should call him."

"If he's coming, he's already on his boat," said Matthew. "And he ain't got no cell with him. Said he's only got but the landline up there."

Peter nodded to himself, but Matthew sensed his unrest.

"Look, you wanna call 'im, then do it," he said.

"You bring your phone with you?" asked Peter.

Matthew shook his head. "Nope. Left it in the truck."

"You're not gonna need it?"

"Wouldn't do me no good leaving it in the truck if I was," Matthew spelled out. He spat off the dock into the black water. "Whatchu hassling me for, anyway? Use your own damn phone."

"Can't," said Peter.

"Why not?" said Matthew.

"Left it in the truck."

The men cackled. They glanced out over the water again. The marbled fog rolled in and enclosed the skeletal oak woods behind them like some supernatural portent. Peter looked towards the eastern treeline, uncannily hazy in the distance. The pale dawn light glowed in a monochrome iridescence as if it were of a higher intelligence, silent and malevolent.

"They say a storm's comin' this weekend," said Peter.

"She ain't hitting 'til Sunday."

Matthew was staring down at the gently rocking dock below him and shook his head.

"Look, you got something to get off your chest, then out with it." Matthew's eyebrows creased. "'Cause I don't want this trailing you the whole weekend. I'm here to hunt and to drink. That's it.

Catch me a big ol' black bear. Not play Name That Tune with you. So, either you buck up and swallow it or you set what's eating you on the table right now before the ferryman gets here."

Peter glanced off, silent for a moment before speaking.

"Alright." Peter nodded to himself. "It ain't sitting with me what we done Tuesday."

Matthew stared forward. "Mm."

"We let him go too far with that boy."

"That boy is in for assaulting his wife. Beats her ass regular. Did you see his files? The state the missus was in when they arrested his ass?" Peter reluctantly nodded. "So, I wouldn't worry too much about him. They're animals, Petey. He's one of *them*. Don't forget that."

"Still. Feels like we up here runnin' or something. Lamming it."

"Yeah? And what we running from?"

"I don't know," said Peter.

"Yeah, well neither do I. And I already done told ya what we up here for. Boozin' and bearin'."

"Uhm."

"Christ, Petey," said Matthew, shaking his head. "Maybe you just getting too soft for the job."

Peter paused. "I think you're right."

Matthew turned to look at him. "Is that a fact?"

Peter nodded. "Think I been done for a while now. Jenny said—"

"Oh, 'Jenny said.' Right. Well, there it is."

"'There it is' nothing. She ain't putting no ideas in my head."

"That's what they all want you to think," said Matthew. "Blinded by the gaslight."

"Oh, you the authority on women now, eh? With your track record?"

"Easy now."

"I'm just saying," Peter looked down.

"Look, you wanna quit, ain't nobody gonna stop ya," said Matthew. "I mean, personally, I think it's the fool's way. You got a good salary, benefits, nice pension waiting up ahead for ya. But hey, that's me. All the same, do me a favor and leave your troubles in the truck as well, would ya? Let it alone this weekend. It'll do you some good to get your mind off things for a while. Besides, Danny says we gettin' a hell of a deal up here, so we might as well try and enjoy ourselves. Said the guy usually charges double what we payin'."

"What makes us so special?"

"Who knows? Who cares," said Matthew. "The owner's been poppin' into Paddy's more and more, chattin' up the regulars, so maybe business ain't been so good. He drops the price to hook himself two good-lookin' SOBs for the weekend!" Matthew winked at Peter.

Peter's mouth gradually broke into a smile. "Yeah, suppose you're right."

"Ain't no supposin' to it."

"Still. That boy, Matty, I just—"

"Hey," Matthew interrupted, tapping Peter on the shoulder. He gestured over the water. "Look."

Through the ghostly murk, a dark apparition emerged. It almost appeared stationary, as if the men were being pulled towards it instead. Its dark iris center grew larger, the dense white gloom diminishing. Like an approaching freight train in a dark tunnel.

Only when the form had come near-parallel with the dock

did the men finally hear the thin clanging of its bow-mounted bell and the low anhedonic moan of its foghorn. It was a small trawler fishing boat, weather-worn and filthy with thick teardrop rust stains running down its façade. A thick wet rope sprung forth from the platform of the boat and bounced off Matthew's chest as it slowed to a stop.

"Tie 'er down, mate," shouted a gruff voice from the bulkhead.

Matthew picked up the rope and wrapped it around the dock cleat. The captain, owner of the island lodge, hopped forth onto the dock with vigor and stood before the men with his hands on his hips. He was a burly man with a bushy salt-and-pepper beard. His thin winter coat was left open to the cold, and he wore a waffled undershirt beneath red flannel. He spat a wad of browned spittle into the water, the inside of his lip thick with chewing tobacco.

The captain extended a gloveless hand to the men.

"Boys. Will Grimley at your service," he said. His grip was firm to the point of intimidation. "This here's my vessel, the *Antigone*."

"Quite a ship," said Matthew, picking up his rifle case and duffel bag.

Will Grimley let out a sharp and boisterous guffaw, startling the men. "Don't patronize me, now. She's a wreck. But then again, ain't we all?"

Matthew grinned and made to board the boat when Will suddenly grabbed him tight around the wrist and pulled him close. Matthew froze. Will was staring deep into his eyes as though searching hard for something.

"Now, I only got one rule for those staying at my lodge," said Will. "Play it straight. No sugar-coatin', no pussyfootin'. Just play it straight. You boys alright with that?"

Matthew smiled uneasily. "Wouldn't have it any other way."

Will looked over at Peter to make sure he was on board.

"Sure, of course," Peter concurred.

Will beamed, bits of black tobacco stuck in his teeth. "Well then, this shapin' up to be a fine weekend, indeed, ain't it? Oh, where are my manners. Here. Let me help you, friend."

Will reached down and picked up Peter's luggage to set it on the boat. He helped the two men board and set to untie the rope from the dock cleat. Matthew and Peter stood in the center of the deck. Then they noticed the presence of a fourth man.

A boy of maybe twenty. He sat on a small bench with his back against the bulkhead, skinning a large dead hare with a bowie knife. He wore a thin blue winter jacket and bright yellow galoshes. He looked up, a vacant grin on his face. The boy's face was crudely disfigured. A large scar swept diagonally down his cheekbone and across his mouth. His nose was craggy and crooked, eyes wide-set. A second hare lay on the bench beside him. Blood and viscera slathered his hands, forearms and the front of his coat, dripping down onto the deck.

Matthew and Peter were agape, eyes unblinking. The boy snorted, his twisted grin deepening, before returning to his work.

Will hopped back onto the platform of the boat with the freed line in his hand and saw the two men stupefied by the boy.

"Oh, that's Bobby, fellas," he said. "Don't mind him. He's born simple, paying for the sins of his father. But he's harmless."

Bobby finished scalping the first hare, its exposed musculature slick with gore. He tossed it whole into a filthy tin bucket in front of him and began to work on the second one. Matthew and Peter glanced at each other before sitting down on the stern bench seat.

"Whelp, what d'ya say? Get this show on the road, huh, boys?" proposed Will. Bobby let out a guttural groan in the affirmative. It sounded almost sexual in its satisfaction.

Peter and Matthew nodded in unison. Will clapped his hands together. "Well, let's go then! All aboard!" He took a couple of steps before pausing and turning. "But first, couple of cold ones in the ice chest there," he gestured behind Matthew and Peter.

Matthew glanced behind him and saw a hatch set into the washboard of the boat. He opened it to reveal six beers sitting in a pool of ice water.

"Unless you two is Protestants or something," said Will.

Matthew reached in and grabbed two beers.

"No, sir. You having one, Will?" asked Matthew.

"Oh, you and I gonna get along just fine, friend." The captain was all smiles, revealing a set of tobacco-stained fangs.

Matthew tossed him a beer and Will caught it, twisting the cap off and handing it to Bobby. Will held his hand up again and Matthew pitched him another bottle to crack for himself.

Bobby held the cold bottle with two hands and tipped it back, taking a long, deep sip. Will followed suit and let out a sigh of pleasure. Peter glanced at young Bobby, who'd already downed half his beer.

"He old enough?" asked Peter.

"Old enough for what?" replied Will.

"To drink."

Will looked over at Bobby and saw him gulping his beer.

"Looks like he's managing it quite capably to me." Will smirked at Peter. He took another sip and looked Peter up and down. "So, you is one of them Proddys, eh?"

"I just meant that we should be careful, in case the Coast Guard shows up." Peter explained.

Will let out another guffaw. "Hoo. Coast Guard? I ain't never seen no guard on this lake in my life. You in God's country now, boys. Subject only to His law. So, drink up."

"Yeah, Petey," said Matthew, handing him a beer. "Drink up."

Peter shrugged. He cracked the beer and took a sip.

"There ya go," cheered Will. "Right as rain."

Will downed the remainder of his beer and pitched the bottle into the black water beyond them. "And awaaaay we go."

He turned around and reversed the engine. The boat slowly backed away from the dock before turning around and heading towards the islet. The boat disappeared into the unholy fog that was now coruscated with the falling snow. Like the dancing ashes of a funeral pyre.

*   *   *

Black Bear Island was about a twenty-five-minute journey away from the dock of Collins Bay. The *Antigone* plowed headlong through the fog. The engine roared with such violence that Peter worried that it might actually blow. Matthew and Peter sat nervously in the back of the boat, trying to raise their beers to their mouths without chipping their teeth.

"Don't worry, boys," screamed Will from the shelter of the bulkhead, staring ahead into the dense brume. "Ol' *Antigone* is used to leading the blind."

He let out a shriek of excitement before abruptly cutting the engine. All fell silent but for the sound of lake water sloshing against the hull. The *Antigone* drifted towards a wooden landing that veered and shifted dramatically in the water, extending far beyond the rocky shoreline of the islet. The boat came parallel with it, and Bobby shot up, hopping onto the dock and expertly tying the back line to the metal cleat. He ran to the front of the boat and Will tossed him the front line, which he tied to the dock as well.

Will turned to face Peter and Matthew, setting his hands on his hips.

"So, boys, what's your business?"

They looked at one another in confusion.

"Your livelihoods," Will clarified. "Your jobs. How you make money. Keep up, now."

"Oh," said Matthew. "We're both custody officers. At the Collins Bay Institution."

"The penitentiary?" Will squinted.

"That's the one," said Peter.

Will stroked his thick beard and nodded his head. "Sounds like that'd be quite interesting."

"It has its moments," replied Matthew, averting his eyes.

Will looked over at Peter and widened his eyes in an animated pantomime. "'Has its moments', says the man." He looked back at Matthew. "I think I'd like to hear about them."

Will then turned and barked over his shoulder, startling the two men. "Bobby! Help these men with their things."

Bobby hurriedly made his way back onto the boat with his head low and grabbed the two overnight bags.

"No, really," said Peter. "We're fine."

"Nonsense," said Will. "You is our guests. Now, shall we?"

He turned to Bobby. "Now don't you forget our lunch neither, boy."

The disfigured boy set the overnight bags on the dock and turned, grabbing the tin bucket that now held the two skinned hares.

The men all climbed onto the crooked dock and began walking towards the shoreline. As the fog thinned near the coast, Peter and Matthew glanced up at the terrain before them. The coastline ascended sharply, a narrow path winding up a densely wooded hillside. Hundreds of thin, lanky white birch trees stood tall above the detritus, their naked arms disappearing into the high brume above. Bobby ran past the men with the two bags and tin bucket at his side, frantically tearing up the winding path towards the top of the hill while making sounds of a revving engine. The sun had risen above the horizon now and mist had set against the grey of the winter morning.

"You boys hear about the storm a-brewin'?" asked Will.

"Yeah, we had," said Peter. "You expectin' it to get bad?"

"Hoo. This is Black Bear Island, son," Will chortled. "Should be interesting."

"Heard it ain't setting down 'til Sunday, though," Matthew chimed in.

"Tomorrow evening, I reckon," said Will. "But that'll give us plenty of time to catch us a set of big ones."

Matthew smiled and glanced around the wooded hillside. "You see a lot of black bears up here?"

"Well, they only named the island after 'em." Will chuckled. "So, yeah. They's a few."

"Ever had any accidents?" asked Peter.

"Accidents. You mean attacks?" A bemused expression was

drawn on Will's face.

"Yeah. Attacks."

"Oh, yeah, you boys best stay close."

"You serious?" Matthew slightly tilted his chin up.

"Serious as a stroke," Will replied. "Lost a few souls last season. Couple cowboys up here gettin' drunk off rot whiskey got all turned around. Fell down a shallow ravine. One must've cut up his leg or something because they didn't last long. A blackie must have sniffed them out. They can smell a carcass from miles off, ya know."

"You were there?" Peter's eyes widened.

"Heavens, no," said Will. "If they was with me they woulda never got lost. I know the isle like the back of my hand. No, I only happened upon the bodies. What was left of 'em, anyway."

There was silence for a moment. Will glanced over at the two men.

"But don't you worry, boys. We gonna have a hell of a time this weekend."

"Quite a few holed up for the season, you reckon?" Matthew inquired.

"Damn good question! Common folks tend not to know this, but blackies differ from their distant cousins to the North in that regard." Will stroked his beard.

"Yeah?"

"Well, not all blackies in these parts hibernate. And those who do, den for shorter periods and they sleep less deeply due to food availability in the area in winter. Roots, fish, small animals, you name it."

"So, we just need to get lucky?" Peter joined in.

"T'is why you boys payin' me the big bucks. I know all of 'em blackies better than my own kin. Their dwellings, habits, hunting grounds…Hell, even their mating preferences," Will chortled. Bobby followed suit.

They emerged at the top of the hill into the greater hinterland. Snow fell softly upon the broad, white flatland that divided the men from two wooden cabins half a mile in the distance. Beyond that, a dense boreal forest covered the rest of the island.

The men trudged on through the ankle-deep snow, eventually arriving at the cabins. Matthew and Peter were surprised to see they weren't rustic hovels, but instead, beautifully constructed cottages. They were luxury hewn-log homes, sided with handcrafted stone chimneys, and wraparound, sheltered porches. Bobby sat on the steps of the cabin to the left, banging a stick against the rail.

"You set these men's things inside?" Will asked.

Bobby nodded vigorously.

"Good boy."

Will held his hand up and Bobby pitched him a set of keys. He caught them and walked Peter and Matthew towards the other cabin. Walking up the steps, Will opened the door and showed the two men inside. It smelled clean and fresh and was free of clutter. The cabin was furnished with a handsome, if outdated, sofa and loveseat upholstered in woolen polyester. The living room had an old boxy television set with a VHS player attached, a stone fireplace, and a handcrafted coffee table. It opened onto an en suite kitchen. Will gestured towards the narrow hallway across from the front entrance.

"You got your two bedrooms down there. Full bathroom and shower. Plenty of hot water, too." He pointed at the television. "TV works just fine, though good luck getting any channels. There's a whole slew of tapes in that cabinet there, though. You'll deduce that I've got an affinity for Westerns."

Peter glanced at the stone fireplace. It was of fine masonry, made from a thick dark granite. He gestured at it.

"That's beautiful," he said.

"Why thank ya." Will held his chest out, chin lifted. "Set it myself."

"No kidding?"

"None. She was some trouble, but you get the right tools and you can bore your way into anything, really. Mold the world to your will." Will winked.

He walked into the kitchen and opened the fridge. It was empty but for a case of beer on the bottom shelf. "Went ahead and got you boys a two-four. On the house, of course, so help yourselves."

"Cheers," Matthew grinned.

"There's a few non-perishables in the cupboards that you're welcome to, but I'll be cooking your meals proper. Fixin' to have a nice rabbit stew for dinner. Be ready in about an hour, so head on over to our place once you get settled."

"Sounds great!" Matthew approved. "Thanks."

"Looks good." Peter was nodding to himself. "Appreciate the hospitality."

Matthew dug into his breast pocket and pulled out a wad of bills and handed them to Will.

"I believe that's what we agreed upon," he said.

"Oh, I'm sure it's all there," Will smirked, pocketing the cash without even looking at it. "Well, I'll let you get acquainted with the cabin here and I'll see you boys in an hour or so?"

"See you in an hour," Matthew agreed, beaming.

"Beautiful," Will whistled.

He tossed Matthew the keys and exited, shutting the door behind him. The two friends looked over the space for a moment and then at each other, still pleasantly surprised with their quarters. They headed to the fridge to crack a beer.

*　*　*

Later on, the four sat at a thick oak table in the small dining room of Will Grimley's cabin. The northern darkness was already upon them, votive candles bounced shadows across the room. The men were drinking stout from glass mugs and eating bowls of hearty rabbit stew. A steaming crock pot stood in the middle of the table beside a fifth of whiskey and four shot glasses.

"God damn, this is delicious," said Peter, finishing another mouthful of stew. He wiped his face with his serviette and glanced over at Bobby. "Oh, pardon my French, Will."

"I didn't hear no French," said Will, smiling over at Bobby. "How 'bout you, Bobs?"

The boy laughed and shook his head, brown dribble running down the side of his mouth.

"No Proddy after all then, eh, Petey?" Will teased, winking at him.

"Where'd you learn to cook like this?" asked Matthew, spooning another mouthful.

"My mama," said Will. "Never really exercised it none until Bobby's kin passed away."

"You two relations?" Matthew paused his chewing.

"Yessir. Bobby here is my nephew. His own mama passed when he was just a young 'un and his daddy—my sorry excuse for a brother—he spent most of his time locked up."

"Really?" Matthew perked up at this. "What's his name?"

"Matt, come on," Peter was slightly shaking his head.

"What?" Matthew looked at him and shrugged.

"Oh, that's right," said Will. "You boys mighta come across him, in your line of work."

"I don't recall any Grimleys though." Matt was rubbing his chin. "Actually, it kinda sounds familiar."

"Yeah, likely not. Son of a bitch changed his name every couple of weeks to avoid the law. Anyways, he livin' out of province. I ain't sure if he ever done time at the CBI. But yeah, now it's just me and the kid here. Nice to finally have some company for the season though, ain't it, Bobby?" Will clapped his nephew hard on the back.

"We your first ones up this year?" Peter inquired.

"Yessir. First victims of the winter."

"You married, Will?" Matthew queried.

"I surely hope not. Else she been gone a real long time!" Will cackled at his own joke.

Matthew joined him.

"How about yourself?" asked Will.

"No. But I was." Matthew was leaning back on his chair. "Didn't last."

"Never does. Kids?"

"One. But…we don't speak much." Matthew looked away.

"Tsk. Shame," said Will. He turned to Peter. "And how about you, Petey?"

"I'm engaged. Getting married next summer." Peter was grinning from ear to ear.

"Oh. Well, now. Congratulations," Will held up his mug and the three others clinked it and drank.

"Thanks." Peter was all smiles.

"You two settin' to have kids of your own?" asked Will.

"Actually," Peter looked over at Matthew beside him, "Jenny's pregnant."

"Really?" Matthew jerked forward. "That's great, man." He slapped Peter on the back.

"Hoo. What news," said Will. He looked over at Bobby. "You hear that, Bobby? This 'un set to have a wee little baby."

Bobby's eyes went wide with glee, spittle falling from his chin.

"Bobby!" screamed Will, shocking the whole table to attention as he slammed his fist against the hard wood. "Wipe yourself. We got company. Where's your manners at, boy?"

Bobby lowered his head and wiped his face with his serviette. Peter and Matthew exchanged glances silently. Will turned back to Peter. His irritation at his nephew seemed to be gone instantly.

"Now this calls for a toast." Leaning forward, Will grabbed the fifth of whiskey, cracked the seal and poured four shots. He held his up. "To our new friend Peter and his fiancée and their wonderful news. May their new blessing always lead them forth from darkness."

The men clinked glasses and drank. Will slapped his hand against the table.

"Hoo, that's good shit!" Will looked at Peter and sneered. Then he turned to Bobby.

"Excusez-moi, Monsieur Bobby," he pouted his lips and

spoke with an exaggerated French accent.

Will looked over at Matthew and Peter's bowls and saw they were near empty.

"You boys help yourselves to seconds, you got room for it."

"Thanks. I think I just might." Matthew ladled himself another bowlful.

"So, tell me a little about your work down there at the pen." Will poured the four of them fresh shots of whiskey. "I am mighty curious. Heard people call it Disneyland North, but I know better. Ain't no maximum-security facility gonna be made up of cotton candy, now, is it?"

"You got that right." Matthew nodded. "People have no idea."

"Ain't that the truth of it." Will puckered his lips. "Of all things."

"CBI is a goddamn zoo!" Matthew scowled. "Incredible violence. Just incredible. On a daily basis. These guys will kill your loved ones, rape your mothers and daughters, take away your life savings without so much as a blink."

"Is that right?" Will raised an eyebrow. "Well, I don't doubt it."

Peter nodded.

"But you don't like to talk about it," stated Will.

"Not particularly." Peter looked down.

"Why's that?"

"Some things you'd just rather leave where they're at."

Will nodded again. "You two wise, I'll give you that."

Peter took a sip of his stout.

"So, how does a man cope?" asked Will. "You'd go crazy in that line of work, I imagine, without some kind of outlet."

"Oh, you take your pleasures where you can find them," Matthew sneered, holding up his stout and taking a sip.

"Yeah, it's tough, though." Peter shook his head. "No getting around it."

"We try to lighten the load up there, though, don't we, Petey." Matthew nudged his friend and chuckled.

"Well, now I'm intrigued." Will tossed his shot of whiskey back and Bobby followed suit.

"Well, for example—" began Matthew.

"Come on, now," said Peter. "Will doesn't want to hear about it."

"Oh, now, that's where you're wrong, friend." Will put his spoon down; there was a sparkle in his eyes.

"Yeah, come on, lighten up, Petey," said Matthew. He looked over at Will. "What happens on the island, stays on the island, right?"

"Couldn't have put it better myself." Will smirked and winked.

Matthew set his spoon down and wiped his mouth and took his shot of whiskey back.

"Well, for example—" Matthew started to lean forward on his elbows before taking another shot back. He lowered his voice to a hush. "We put the new blood through training."

"Training, hm?" Will made a sucking noise.

"Oh yeah. Lil' something we like to call 'schooling'. I mean, a new inmate gets thrown on your block, you have to show them you mean business, right? That they can't fuck around. That you're the one running the program. Or else it's just total anarchy."

"So what's the program? This…'schooling'?" Will picked up the whiskey bottle and refilled everybody's shot glasses.

"In a word? Gilles."

"'Gilles', huh? Well, pardon your French, Matthew," Will chortled.

"Gilles the Giant," Matthew continued. "This humongous French-Canadian motherfucker. Serving consecutive life sentences. Fists like phone books. So, what we do is—" Matthew paused to take his shot. Peter frowned, nibbling his lower lip. "About a week or so after the newbies come in, we move them to a vacant cell in the prison basement. A disused block now. Nobody there. That place gives me the creeps, man. Even after all these years. And then we let Gilles the Giant loose on them."

Peter shifted uncomfortably in his seat. "Hey, come on. We really shouldn't be talking about this."

"Oh, Petey," said Will. "Don't be embarrassed. Trust me, living up here, in the harsh wilderness, tracking bears for a living—I know the monster's nature can spawn. And if you don't claim dominion over your territory, you'll get swallowed whole by 'em. It's a dirty business, but it's life, right, Matty? Dog eat dog."

"Exactly," said Matthew. "See, Petey, he gets it."

"Now don't leave me hangin', friend." Will was looking at Matthew with big, wide eyes. "What's ol' Gilles the Giant get up to?"

"Whatever the hell he wants." Matthew laughed, taking back another shot.

"Physically? Sexually? What?" Will was close to salivating at this point.

"You just have to witness it yourself," Matthew leered. "He can be pretty creative, I must say."

"God damn. You seen it?"

"Seen it? Hell yeah. We gotta make sure he doesn't go overboard." Matthew shrugged. "So, yeah, one of us always stays down there to keep watch. But let me tell you something, when those first-timers come back up on the block, they're as docile as newborn fawns."

"I bet. Ever had any accidents?" Will's eyes were glinting in the soft yellow light.

"You mean attacks?" asked Matthew.

"I mean deaths."

Peter cleared his throat and Will looked over at him.

"Seems like you want to get one specific off your chest, Petey." Will was stroking his beard.

Peter looked over at Will and then at Matthew. He grabbed the bottle of whiskey and refilled his glass.

"It went too far this past Tuesday," he said, taking his shot. "Gilles nearly killed some poor kid."

"Poor kid? You keep saying that." Matthew turned to Will. "Petey here acting like the boy was some saint. He was a violent predator. In and out of the slammer before he got his zits. They don't learn."

"You do this to all the new inmates?" Will inquired.

"Pretty much, yeah," said Matthew. "Kind of the way it goes down there."

Will got up and enthusiastically poured them all more shots. Peter shook his head, but Will poured him some anyway.

"This is gettin' exciting. Like watchin' one of those true-crime documentaries. I like it. Tell me more! You guys got no piece of the action? Just stand and watch? Come on, now. I ain't buyin' that!" Will's eyeballs were close to popping out of their sockets.

"Not re—"

"Course we do," Matthew cut Peter short. He seemed a little tipsy, his eyes glazed. "It's all part of the job. You gotta know that jail time is way too good for some of these motherfuckers. They're real monsters. Somebody gotta keep them in line. It's our lives on the line, at the end of the day."

"They're not exactly harmless, huh?" Will sympathized.

"One time, there's these savage twins. Ex-MMA fighters. They beat up this kid in the shower. Two guards tried to stop them but got ass-kicked instead. One of them lost an eye. Had to retire."

"Animals!" Will banged his glass against the table.

"They fucking brag about that and keep making troubles. So we figure, we have to break them up. We starved them for days, just enough water to keep them functional. We told them whoever gives in first will get bread and be exempt from a session with Gilles. The younger brother tapped out, cried like a little girl. Elder brother didn't exactly enjoy his honeymoon with Gilles." Matthew sniggers.

"What happened to the brothers?"

"They didn't speak for months. Younger 'un ended up getting shanked and died. Wonder who ordered the hit!" Matthew grinned. He carried on, "We're in the business of match-making too!"

"Oh? How noble," Will muttered.

"Yeah, of course. We value friendship as much as law and order! Petey, you remember Lane and…what's his face?"

"Burt," Peter finished. He looked a little pale.

"Yeah, Burt! What a dick! Lane and Burt were cellmates. Hated each other's guts, kept trying to waste the other. Anyway, they kept getting into fights, recruiting other inmates for their personal vendetta, creating mayhem and unrest. One day, we stormed into their cell and moved them to a cell in the abandoned wing. We stripped 'em naked. There's no mattress, no bedding in there, nothing. Not even toilet paper. This was in January, mind you. The coldest season these parts had seen since the Gold Rush. Lying on that freezing concrete floor, they had to brave the cold, with nothing between their naked skin and the wrath of winter."

"That's cold! Literally." Will downed his drink quickly, as though he could feel the chill creeping into his bones.

"A couple of hours later, guess what we found?"

"Frozen buns?" guessed Will. Bobby covered his face and snorted.

"Two nearly-hypothermic, shivering Siamese twins lying on the floor. Limbs tangled, teeth chattering, balls enmeshed. Trying to get as much skin contact as possible with each other. That was quite a sight. Like a couple who'd been separated for too long, making up for lost time and memories." Matthew finished his story with a flourish one would find in a poem reading.

"Whew…that's a lot to take in. That worked? They quit fightin'?"

"Yeah. We captured their indecent moments from every angle and told them we would distribute the photos amongst the inmates if they so much as looked the other the wrong way."

"You ain't worried about gettin' caught?" Will was rubbing his clean-shaven chin.

"By who? The warden sees the shape our block is in. Barely any fights, the men obey the guards, everything running smooth. So, he don't ask. But of course, he ain't stupid. He knows something is keeping them animals in line. But what he don't know can't hurt him."

Matthew poured another shot. "Besides, you get used to the whole thing. It's the program, right? After a while, all the new recruits start looking the same anyways. Can't tell one from the other. So, it's just part of the job at this point, really. Just something you do."

"Hoo," said Will. "You boys really are something. But you're exactly right. Them kind of criminals need to know the score. Lock them up and throw away the key, that's what I say. CBI is for the most dangerous predators in the country, so all the power to you. After all, if they gonna break the law on the outside, why should they be disciplined lawfully on the inside?"

"You looking for a job, Will?" Matthew sniggered. "'Cause we could use more fellas like you on the block."

Bobby let out a loud cackle, mimicking Matthew, and chugged the rest of his stout.

Will looked over at his nephew with dead, serious eyes. Bobby stopped laughing, mouth agape. Will's facial features softened, and he let out a booming shriek of laughter. That got the boy going again, much louder this time.

"Well, way I look at it," said Will, "what you boys dishin' out is just a taste compared to the pain and suffering those animals have inflicted upon their victims. If you ask me, you boys deserve some goddamn medals! You doin' God's work, really."

"Hear, hear," cried Matthew. Peter reluctantly echoed him.

The shots were refilled, and Will raised a toast to the men. They all shouted cheers and emptied their glasses. Will then picked the near-empty bottle back up and swished it in his hand.

"What d'ya say, boys? Shall I crack open another?"

*　*　*

The boreal wilderness of the island was vast and hilled, its northern side ending in a rocky bluff that jutted violently out of the lake water below. Thick cloths of untouched, white mountain ash collected upon the coniferous trees, white spruce and jack pines seemed to ebb and flow into the distance like some hallucinatory taiga's cape. The mid-morning sun hung bright in the sky. And though it remained overcast, it was nevertheless a picturesque setting for their virginal bear hunt.

The four men trudged across a shallow valley of snow-covered rock at a slow pace, all carrying their hunting rifles. Will had spotted whitetail tracks at the mouth of the valley and suggested they follow. If they could track a deer and kill it and cut it open, he said, a bear would be sure to follow the scent, so long as the men remained out of sight.

Matthew and Peter tailed the party and struggled to keep up, viciously hungover from having drank late into the night the day prior. Matthew stopped to lean against a boulder and titled his head up, taking in the fresh winter air while messaging his temples.

Will, his underlip packed with chewing tobacco, noticed the two lagging behind. He stopped and backtracked with Bobby. Peter stood on a rock near Matthew, the butt of his rifle leaning against his thigh. Will nodded at him as he came near.

"You hard as nails, Petey," Will commended with a wink. He looked towards Matthew. "Matty, on the other hand, lookin' like he might need some hair of the dog."

Will came upon Matthew and lowered his rifle and reached into his jacket pocket. He pulled out a steel flask and handed it to Matthew. Matthew looked at it a moment, eventually taking it and took a swill. He then let out a deep groan.

"That'll cure ya, right good." Will grinned.

Will turned and tossed the flask up to Peter. He caught it but held his hand up in refusal.

"I'm good," he said.

"You be a whole lot better with some of that moonshine in ya," said Will.

Peter looked at Will and then over at Matthew, who nodded. "It's packing a wallop."

Peter shrugged. He removed the cap and took a swig. He went white and coughed hard and Bobby began laughing perversely, nearly asthmatic in his glee.

Peter tossed the flask back down to Will and he put it away.

"Ain't you having one?" said Peter.

"It's ten o'clock in the morning, boys," Will said with a smirk. "I ain't no alkie."

The men continued on and soon emerged out of the valley; the whitetail tracks still before them. They tracked the deer across a flat meadow and through the dense brushland beyond it before Will held up his fist and signaled for the men to stop. Will slowly dropped to one knee and Bobby followed suit. Will waved for the two men to come closer. They came upon him, and Will gestured ahead. Deep within the woods stood a large whitetail buck sniffing the ground.

"She's all yours, boys," whispered Will. "Quickly now."

Peter looked over at Matthew and Matthew gestured for him to take the shot.

"I can barely see straight." Matthew shook his head.

Peter crouched behind a thick rotten log and set up behind it. He set the barrel of his rifle across it and slowly, soundlessly unclicked the safety and checked his sight. The buck was dead-set in the center of his scope.

Peter took a moment, a breath, exhaled, and squeezed. The

sound echoed out over the hinterland and into the great beyond. When Peter looked up, the whitetail was lying on the snow in the distance. A clean kill shot right through the neck.

"Hoo!" said Will, rising to his feet. "You a goddamn sniper, boy."

Bobby clapped his hands together hard in a jerked rhythm, cackling with glee.

Matthew rose and looked ahead at the dead deer and over at Peter. There was now a widening halo of red just under its head. Both men were wide-eyed with exhilaration.

"Welp, let's go on and get at that carcass," said Will.

Bobby stood up and pulled out his bowie knife from his belt sheath. Peter smiled and headed across to the deer but stumbled after a few steps. He stopped walking and shook his head slightly. He tried to continue but nearly fell over, steadying himself against a tree.

"You alright there, pal?" Will sounded concerned.

Matthew took a step forward to help his friend, but his knees quivered and he too stumbled. With nothing to hold on to for support, Matthew dropped to one knee, trying to shake it off. He looked up and saw Will staring down at him emotionlessly.

Peter held himself up with the tree and glanced over at Bobby. He was prowling towards them with a perverted Cheshire Cat grin on his face, the serrated bowie knife at his side. Peter held up his hand but collapsed to the ground at nearly the same moment Matthew did. And all went black.

*　*　*

Peter awoke first. His eyes took nearly a minute to adjust, the space darkened and alien. He smelled the place, cold and damp and rotten. Something metallic. Aluminum, maybe. And a sweet, putrid reek. He felt the rocky ground around him. It was wet and filthy. He shook his head and stared again and soon his focus sharpened. A dim orb of white light shone beside him at the far end of a tunnel. He was stuck in some shallow mine, he thought. He turned and saw Matthew out cold beside him, slumped against a rock. Naked.

Peter realized that he was, too. Not a piece of cloth covering their nudeness. A breeze of cold air made him shudder. He attempted to stand but felt the tug of his ankle. He looked down and saw he was shackled in a metal handcuff connected to a thick chain. He followed the chain to its end and saw that it was held by an iron ring bored into the rockface of the cave.

"It's in there good," Will spoke. "No use thinkin' about yankin' her clear."

Peter turned and squinted into the darkness and saw Will leaning against a boulder, all but invisible in the dim light. Bobby sat on the rock floor at his feet, slick with blood, smearing his clothes. Peter saw the carcass of the whitetail buck before them and recoiled. It lay completely hairless, its musculature exposed.

Bobby hacked off the last of its skin with his bowie knife. The eyeless, ghastly deer face stared back at Peter.

"Where the hell are we?" Peter panicked. "What's going on?"

"Now, now. Save your strength," said Will. "You're in a bear cave."

Peter looked around and tugged at his ankle. "What the heck, Will? Let us go!"

"Calm yourself, Petey."

Peter shook Matthew beside him, and Matthew groaned

deeply, still very out of it.

"What the hell you give us?" Peter scowled.

"Oh, my own concoction."

"Did you poison us?"

"In a manner of speaking, yes. But the worst of it's over now. Worst of the drugging, anyway."

Bobby hacked off one of the legs of the whitetail with his bowie knife and tossed it between Matthew and Peter. The meat plopped onto the rock floor with a loud wet echo. Blood splattered onto Peter's chest. He shrieked and jerked backwards.

"Why are you doing this?" Peter shouted. "I—I don't understand."

"What you confused about, friend?"

"I—why…"

"Why have I shackled you and your buddy inside a bear cave?"

"Yes. That." Peter glanced towards the dim light of the cave mouth in the distance. The soft ivory glow swathed the rugged walls of the cave mouth.

"Yeah, that's right. They'll be by before long, soon as they get a scent of this." Will gave Bobby a sign with his hand.

Bobby plopped down another piece of reeking deer meat onto the cave floor.

"What the fuck is going on?" Peter's face was as white as a sea-bleached shell.

"Figure since you two boys liked playing God so much, 'bout time you be on the receiving end." Will spat out his tobacco.

"What's—I don't know what that means." Matthew stirred beside Peter. "Wake up, Matty!" Peter kicked Matthew's foot. A groan.

"Bobby?" said Will. "Set upon our friend here."

Bobby instantly shot forward, crawling like some tarantular demon, the bowie knife clutched in his grip. He burst upon Peter, who turned away and shut his eyes in fear. Bobby held still, inches from his face. Peter gulped.

"Look at him," said Will. "Come on, now. Open your eyes."

Peter did and slowly turned his head back to look at Bobby. His hair was matted in blood, his face scrawled in viscera, his smile profane, as if he'd just been birthed by a forgotten angel.

"Do you recognize him?" said Will.

Peter held silent, in shock with the entire situation.

"Do you recognize him, Petey? It's a simple question."

"I—like from before yesterday?"

"Yessir," said Will.

"No. No, I don't recognize him."

Will nodded. "Alright, Bobby. Back to work."

Just as quick as he came, Bobby scrambled back over to Will's feet, glaring at Peter. After a moment, he went back to the carcass. Then he began to enthusiastically scatter slabs of raw meat throughout the cave while humming a tune. Just a child of God reveling in his little sunflower patch.

"They all start looking the same to you after awhile, huh?" said Will to Peter. "Well, granted, his face did look quite different before. So, I guess that's understandable."

"Oh, no…" Peter moaned.

"You boys sure did drink a lot last night," said Will. "Forgot to mention that Bobby here was in CBI," Will said, matter-of-factly. Peter turned towards Will. "Block D, block of death they call it, that's you guys, ain't it?"

Peter's eyes blinked rapidly; his face grew pale. He was not liking where this was going.

Peter's jaws dropped to the ground. "We…"

"That's right. I see you connect the dots real quick. Bobby here's one of the victims of your notorious schooling program. You see, as I mentioned, my brother was a fuckup. A career criminal. And a couple years back he took his son Bobby to a liquor store robbery. Bobby here was the getaway driver. But the car wouldn't start. These dreadful winters of ours, huh? So his father just bailed on foot. Left his motherless son there. And Bobby had just turned eighteen, so, no juvey for him. Off he went to the CBI. Into the hands of you two soulless fucks."

Will spat out another gob of tobacco. Bobby giggled stupidly.

"Used to be a sweet, bright kid," said Will. "Funny too. Man, he was hilarious. Until you two fed him to Gilles the Giant. That monster bashed his head in, collapsed his skull. Did all this to his face. And Bobby ain't never been the same since. Never will be again."

"Please, Will," pleaded Peter. "Please. I'm sorry!"

"Save it, son," said Will.

"I've got a kid on the way."

"You think Bobby here will have a kid some day? Someone acceptin' who he is now? To hold and love him? No, sir. That's beyond even God's hands."

Peter shoved Matthew hard. "Wake up!" Matthew groaned again and started to come to, groggily looking around himself.

"Matt, wake up!" screamed Peter.

"What the…" Matthew glared at the pieces of meat and blood trails.

"They wanna hurt us, Bobby here was under our care!" Peter quickly brought Matthew up to speed. Matthew looked utterly baffled. Peter might as well be speaking Russian.

Peter enthusiastically pointed to Bobby with his free hand. "We did that!" Matthew blinked a few times. Then his face darkened as it sank in.

"Listen, you two," Will uttered, fishing a metallic key out of his coat pocket and holding it out for Peter and Matthew to see. "This is important. Bobby hid one of these inside the carcass."

Peter turned back to Will in horror and stared at what remained of the whitetail's corpse between them. He'd been gutted up the middle, his insides spilling out onto the cave floor. Bobby cackled as he wiped his mouth, smearing a streak of blood across his face. Sitting up, Matthew now had a good grip of their dire situation but was still consumed by grogginess. He drunkenly tugged at his ankle and moaned, trying to speak, only producing vowels.

"It's…in th-there?" Peter stammered.

"Yessir," said Will.

"Wha—what you gonna do with the other key?"

"Oh, I'm gonna hold onto this one for the time being." Will dramatically put the key back into his breast pocket.

"So…only one of us can possibly get out of here?"

"That's right. Boy, you a sharp one."

"Whoever gets himself free—should you find the key, that is—is gonna have to leave the other one behind," said Will. "And should the finder find the key that's not for his cuffs, well, he gets to decide if he's gonna die alone or with a friend. Either way, if I were one of yous, I'd want to find the key ahead of the other lad. Trust me."

Peter again futilely pulled at his ankle shackle, tugging in desperation. The light of the cave mouth strobed, and Peter darted his head towards it. It had begun to snow hard now, the precipitation striating the daylight.

Will glanced towards the cave mouth. "Yeah, storm's coming in good now. And them blackies likely be picking up the scent of this whitetail by now." Will rubbed his hands together.

"Tell you what, the one of you able to set himself free and find his way across the island to the dock, in this storm, without clothes on his back? Hell, I might even consider taking him home myself. That'd be some feat."

"Will, please," begged Peter. "I know you're angry, but you can't do this. Please! We were just doing our job! I'm getting married!"

Peter began to weep.

"Yeah, well, I had a nephew once," said Will. He stared down at Bobby. "A sweet boy. And look what you two done to him. Who's gonna give him his life back?"

"Please, Will! You can escort us two to the county station. We will confess to everything. Please! I'm sorry!" Matthew chimed in.

"Turn yous in? Hoo. So, what, they can lock me up? No, I seen how the law work on Bobby already. It protects its own."

"Bobby!" Peter turned. "Bobby…please. I—"

Bobby stared back blankly, twisting his head in curiosity. Like a dog being shown a card trick.

Will chuckled. "Nice try. He has a bit of difficulty registering human emotion since his time at the CBI, you understand."

Tears streamed down Peter's cheeks. With bloodshot eyes, he faced Matthew. "This is all your fault! Blabbermouth! Look what you did, moron!"

"Yeah well, you got me the job and Gilles was OUR idea! Don't be denying your part in all of this!"

"Welp," Will interrupted. "'Bout time Bobby and I be shoving off. Matthew, Peter. I bid you adieu. Can't say it's been a pleasure. But this will heal some. C'mon now, Bobby!"

The two began towards the cave mouth. Will paused and looked back. "Better start digging, boys." He saluted and kept walking.

Peter screamed after them. Matthew soon joined in. Their cries were unintelligible, like that of some extinct and unfamiliar species. The wailing and the sound of chain clinking echoed off the cavern walls as the two guards lunged and jostled for the carcass.

Will and Bobby emerged from the cave into the worsening day. The sky was grey and rotting, the snow falling hard across that hinterland. The cries of the two men inside were barely audible now.

Will reached into his mouth and pulled out the used wad of chewing tobacco and tossed it to the ground. He took out his tin and opened it and packed a fresh wad behind his lip and set the lid back on the tin again. Bobby stared over at him, looking between Will and the tin. Will grinned and took the lid off again and offered the tin to Bobby. Tongue in the side of his mouth, Bobby took a pinch and packed it behind his lip like he'd seen Will do time and time again.

Will spit some of the juice out and Bobby followed suit and smiled up at Will. But after a moment, Bobby turned green and retched into the snow beside him. He reached into his mouth and pulled the entire tobacco wad out and threw it down. Will guffawed. Bobby looked at him and burst out laughing, drool hanging off his chin, his teeth speckled with tobacco grind. Almost the entire body was slathered up in gore and bloodied pieces of innards.

The winter sky rumbled with a low thunder. Miles off, but coming in quick. Will glanced out over the island and nodded to himself.

"Them bears gonna be lookin' to shelter themselves now," said Will.

Bobby nodded and beamed.

Will reached into his breast pocket and pulled out two identical metal keys. He held them in the palm of his hand in front of Bobby.

"Your honor, buddy," Will spoke.

Bobby looked at him and then at the two keys. He picked them up.

His face was solemn. Eyes moist. For a split second, they flickered.

Behind them, the scent of the carcass wafted from the mouth of the cave as the storm rolled in from the west, bristling with cold fury and malevolence.

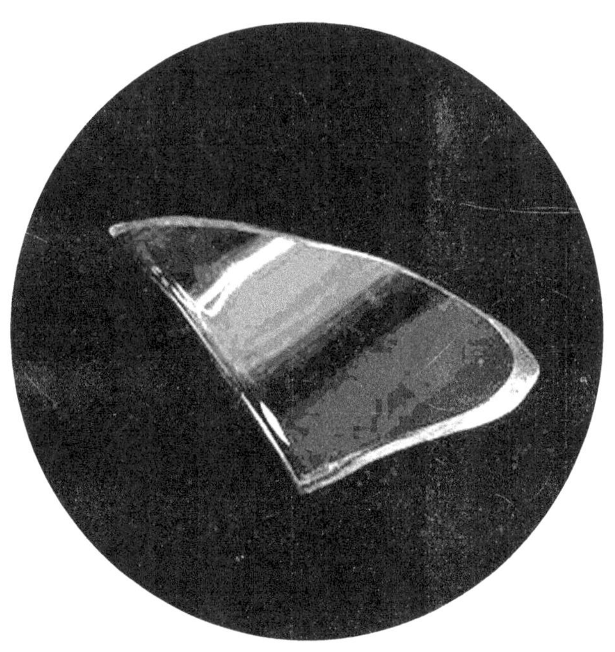

BLUE DEVILS

I lean forward awkwardly, trying to apply the blood-red lipstick as I peer at my own reflection in the cracked mirror propped against my dressing room wall.

My fingers tremble slightly. Feeling a little giddy. Shouldn't have drunk. Oh God, Leon will be here too!

Get it together, Savi! I reassure myself, inhaling deeply. You go onstage in ten.

Trying to rehearse while still saving my voice, I hum one of my numbers softly. As I gaze at the medium-statured woman in the large mirror, I can't help but wonder where the years have gone. Big grey eyes stare back at me with blatant exhaustion.

I have been singing here since I was a teenager, and little about this pub has changed. But after almost a couple of decades, I have to acknowledge that I see a definite change in myself. The imperceptible stooping of the shoulders, the waning of hair luster, the diminishing glow of the face and eyes. The once-happy, energetic idealist of my youth has become faded and disillusioned. I was a fighter, a survivor. Now it feels as though I'm just going through the motions.

I notice that the dark circles underneath my eyes are visible, even through my foundation. In the dim lighting, I look like a mere shadow of my old self.

My dressing room is really nothing more than a dingy little storage room in the back of the bar. But to me, it's the center of my world as a performer. Three times a week, I can be found here, getting ready to go onstage. But what had once felt like a second home to me is now beginning to feel like a jailhouse.

I hear the door open without a knock. I turn my head. At the sight of a familiar shark-like grin, I tense. It's Tony, my ex. He saunters in and shuts the door.

The room turns cold. It's suddenly hard to breathe.

No! This can't be happening!

"Wh-What are you doing here?" I try to hide the quivering in my voice. I can't believe he would violate the restraining order just like this.

Tony shrugs as though he owns the place. I scowl.

"Aww, Vanna Bear, I miss you too!" he mocks. "Aren't you going to give me a kiss?"

"The only thing I'm going to give you is two minutes to leave before I call the cops," I warn. Turning back to the mirror, I track his reflection as he stalks the room behind me.

"Don't be like that, baby," he whines. "I'm not here to cause any trouble, I just need a favor."

I give a heavy sigh.

"I don't have any money, Tony." I pause as he draws close behind me.

"Come on, all I need is a twenty for gas." I can feel his heat as he rests his big hands on my tiny shoulders. "Come on. For old time's sake?" My fear spikes as he deliberately slides his hands toward my throat.

"Fine." Breaking away, I collect my purse and withdraw my wallet. Trying not to let Tony see inside, I turn around as I riffle through the contents of the wallet, taking out a twenty-dollar bill.

"Here." I thrust it at him. "Now will you just go?"

Tony snatches it from me, chortling.

"Hey, thanks." He gives me a measuring look.

"Say…you sure you don't got any more to spare?"

"Get out of here, Tony!" I yell, finally losing my composure. "Go get a job for once! Just leave me alone!"

His eyes narrow, and I take a step back. "Don't you talk to me like that, you bitch! All I want is a little cash. I know you've got it." He advances on me. "Gimme that wallet."

"No!" I try to shove it back into my purse, but Tony snatches it away from me. He extracts all the cash from it and casually drops the wallet onto the floor. I lash forward, reaching out to take the thin wad of bills away from his clutch.

"You'd better stop it, bitch, or do I have to remind you what an ass-whooping feels like?" He has a hold of my wrists now, squeezing them so tightly I can feel my bones grinding together.

"Bet you miss it," he teases as I cringe and try to pull away.

Suddenly, there's a knock on the door. Both of us are rooted to the spot.

"Five minutes 'til showtime, Savannah!" It's Daisy, the bartender.

"I'll be right there!" I call back, hoping that my voice sounds normal.

Tony finally lets go, brushing himself off with a chuckle.

"Your audience awaits, my love," he sneers.

I rub my wrists gingerly, stepping back over to the mirror to finish getting ready.

"Leave, Tony. I swear to God, if you ever come back, I will call the cops."

"Alright, alright," he says, putting his hands up. Tony steps away, obviously happy enough with the cash. He strolls toward the door.

"See ya around, Vanna Bear."

As soon as I hear the door shut behind him, I collapse. Gasping with sobs, I crawl over to my purse, shoving a hand inside to grope for the little metal container that has lately been starting to feel like my sole salvation.

There! I pull it out, looking down at the tiny, hinged box. I get up, staggering. Opening the box, I hurriedly shake out some of the white powder within, onto the back of my hand. Then, holding one nostril closed, I snort it up. The rush hits me shortly after.

Panting, I gaze at my own reflection in the mirror and stare at the wild-eyed woman looking back at me, her long black hair a tangled mess. I don't even recognize *her*.

*   *   *

My voice rings out strong and clear as I finish the final act. After a brief pause, the room springs into applause. Although the bar is half-empty, the patrons seem thrilled at the performance.

"Thank you! Thank you, everyone." I smile appreciatively. "Thanks for coming out. You've been a great audience." I bow a few times. I notice a man standing toward the back of the room, his gaze intent on me. My smile slips for a moment when I notice how his eyes burn, unwavering. Then he slips out through the exit.

A loud whistle distracts me. I mumble several more thank yous to the patrons and the jazz band, then wearily step down from the stage. I walk over to the table located front and center.

Leon stands up, his bright white grin shining in the dim light. He gives me a warm hug and I fold into his arms. Leon may not be the most effective agent, but he is certainly the most supportive.

"You were great up there, Savi!" His brown eyes sparkle, his handsome mahogany visage beaming. "Your performance was perfect. And you look beautiful tonight."

I blush, self-consciously stroking my hair.

"Yeah right, I'm a mess. But thanks!"

"No, I mean it!" he says earnestly. "I'm sorry I haven't been able to get you into more clubs lately. The city's pretty saturated with talent right now. But a one-of-a-kind jazz singer like you deserves to be heard."

"It's all right, Leon," I reassure him. "I know it's tough out there. I do appreciate everything you've done for me, though."

Pulling out a chair, Leon ushers me to sit down at the table. As he motions for the bartender to bring me a drink, I grin. His lanky frame is draped in an inexpensive suit, but he still stands out among all the men in the bar.

Leon has been representing me for quite some time now. I have gone from a rising star with a record deal destined to bring us both success, to a hopeless addict and serial battered girlfriend. But through it all, he stands by me with unwavering support and encouragement. I don't know how I can ever repay him.

"Thanks," I say when a waitress sets my apple martini down in front of me. Taking a sip, I smirk at Leon. "What would I do without you?”

He chuckles, looking to the side. “Something tells me you’d land on your feet. You’re the strongest woman I’ve ever met, Savi. No matter what the world throws at you, you’re going to survive it. I have no doubt of that.”

“Thanks, Leon.” I smile and he gazes at me for a moment, as though transfixed. I take another sip of my drink, trying to hide my blush.

“You know…” I start, clearing my throat. “I hope you don’t feel like you have to come to see my performances so much. You must be busy with the other singers you’re representing.”

“Nonsense,” Leon insists, putting his hand over mine. The warmth of his steady palm emanates to my hand. “I enjoy watching you. This is my break from work. You taking that away from me now?”

I chuckle.

“You’re a once-in-a-generation singer, Savi. I know things might be tough right now, but they’ll improve. I’ll never stop believing that.” He grins. “Besides, I’m counting on you to take me with you when you hit the big time.”

We laugh together, relaxed in each other’s company. The bar is starting to empty out now as the night wanes.

“I mean, I wish you could hear yourself the way I hear you,” Leon continues, his voice animated. “I’m blown away by your performance every single night, without fail.”

I sip my drink; my good mood begins to fade. It’s hard to believe in such effusive praise, given the situation, even from my agent and friend. If I’ve learnt anything from my past broken relationships, it’s that nice words and gestures are seldom given freely.

"Is there any news on other gigs?" I ask, hopeful.

"Well, there might be something on the horizon that's a little better than most," Leon responds, pulling out his phone. "I'll send you the contact information of a venue manager. He wants to meet you in person. It's a venue that's opening soon and they're looking for talent to create a regular lineup."

I nod enthusiastically, feeling excited. At this point, I would embrace any kind of change of scenery. I think it'd be good for me, a fresh start. Even though I know fully well that the grass is not always greener on the other side.

"Thank you so much, Leon." I feel a pang of guilt. "I'm embarrassed that I've been behind lately on giving you your cut of the last couple of gigs. I'll pay you back as soon as I can, I promise."

"No worries." He smiles, leaning forward, a serious expression on his face. "But be fully prepared for me to collect, with interest and all, once you're a superstar!"

"Deal." I nod my head and wink.

"I believe in you, Savi," Leon reminds me. "Don't you forget that. If anyone's got what it takes to be successful in this business, it's you."

For some reason, though I detect sincerity in his voice, I feel alone.

"I doubt I'll be able to aspire to anything more than survival at this point," I say wistfully. "I had my shot but blew it. As far as superstardom is concerned, that ship has sailed."

Leon looks at me, eyes a little pensive. After putting some money down on the table to cover our bill, he escorts me out to my car.

"Listen." His hands rest on my shoulders as we stand by my

old beaten-up sedan. The cool night wind flutters my long hair. "Whatever happened in your past, whether it has to do with your career or your personal life…you can't put that on yourself. You don't deserve to carry it like a burden." His brown eyes stare intently into my grey ones. "You need to make peace with yourself. Give yourself permission to be happy."

I can feel a mocking grin stretch across my face, born from the insecurity in my heart. "'Give myself permission to be happy?' What, did you get that out of a self-help book?"

When I see the hurt on Leon's face, I immediately regret it. I look away, ashamed.

"Anyway…if I weren't such a sad sack then I wouldn't be so good at singing the blues, right?" I kick a piece of parking lot gravel away with my toe. The yellow streetlights throw strange patterns of lights and shadows across the lot. There is silence between us for a minute. I'm deflated. Leon is the last person on earth I mean to hurt.

"I'm sorry." I look back at his face, feeling tears pricking at the corners of my eyes. "It's been a hard stretch."

Leon nods, putting his hands in his pants pockets.

"It's alright, Savi." He watches me as I fumble for the door of my car and slide inside. "I'll always be here for you. Believe in that, if nothing else." He hesitates for a second, then adds, "You know how I feel about you."

I clutch the wheel with both hands, a lump forming in my throat.

I'm afraid that ship has sailed too.

I mumble my goodbye, quickly drive off, and don't look back.

Eyes glazed with dammed waterworks, I stare silently ahead the whole drive home. I don't even bother to turn on the radio to my favorite station, like I usually do. I just watch the interplay of city lights through my windshield, reflecting on all the years that have passed me by.

*   *   *

Back at my apartment, I drop my purse on the kitchen table with a sigh. Feels like I'm chained to a giant boulder. I'm constantly letting Leon down. Whatever I'm giving him, it's not enough. He deserves better. Despite his seemingly unwavering support for me, there'll be a time when he decides enough is enough. And I wouldn't blame him. I'd have fired my ass years ago if I were him.

I'm not holding my breath for the new prospective gig either. I've been bested way too often by less-talented—albeit younger and prettier—singers to hold out any hope.

I dawdle to the sofa and slump down. Silently, I stare at the discolored square on the wall where my television had once sat. I had a break-in a couple of months earlier and they'd taken the TV, along with several personal items. The emptiness of my apartment is starting to resemble the futility of my existence.

The bottle of pills I keep in my medicine cabinet springs to mind. I hold onto them because most days it makes me feel better to know that I have an out, even if I don't take it. But tonight, I'm comforted by their presence for a much darker reason.

Trying to put the thoughts out of my head, I take a shower. Standing under the hot spray, I reflect on that night and the ones before it. No matter how often I've been told that I have a unique voice, or that I am worth something, I find it difficult to believe. I mean, just look at the state of my career, my life.

Finally turning off the water, I wring out my wet hair and plait it into a long rope. Stepping over to the sink, I pause, considering my wan face in the dim light of the tiny bathroom. I look worn, insignificant. Like an old baseball glove, collecting dust in the attic.

Slowly, I open the medicine cabinet. Reaching inside, my hand quickly finds the bottle. I stand and contemplate it for a minute. A seemingly innocuous little orange cylinder. The label has long since been ripped off and discarded.

Hurriedly, worried that I may lose resolve, I open the bottle and down the contents in one gulp. I chase the pills with water from the sink. Then I find myself glaring in the mirror. In shock. What have I done?

Suddenly, Leon's beaming face jolts to mind. When I don't show up tomorrow, who will come to check on me? He will.

At the thought of Leon finding my cold body, I stagger toward the toilet, shoving two fingers down my throat. Violently, I puke out the pills, making sure not to stop until nothing comes up but bile.

Coughing and gasping for air, I slump down on the bathroom floor for a while, undecided whether to laugh or cry that, once again, I will live to see another day.

After what seems like hours, I finally get up and make my way back towards the kitchen. Going through my purse, I pull out my little metal box with a sense of inevitability. No matter what, I always end up back in the same place.

Shaking out a line of snowy, luscious talc onto the kitchen table, I lean over and let the rush take me.

*   *   *

A few days later, Leon texts me for an update on the gig he was telling me about. To be honest, I've forgotten all about it. It seems like a long shot, but what do I have to lose?

Pulling out my phone, I find the contact Leon had sent me in our text thread. "Manager" is all that's listed in the name field. Curious, I send him a text.

Hi, this is Savannah. I think you know my agent, Leon?

It couldn't have been more than a minute before I hear the ding of a response.

Yes, I know you.

I wait a moment for further messages, but there is nothing. I type out a response.

Leon told me you're looking to audition singers for your new club?

I wait hopefully. Moments later, another text.

I have seen you perform. I'm very interested in you. I want you to come sing for me.

I nearly jump with exultation. Looks like I have this one in the bag!

Of course! I text back. *Just name the time and place.*

After a brief pause, I receive an address.

Come at noon.

This reply gives me pause. Noon? It's already past eleven o'clock. No matter, I want this.

I text back my agreement to meet the venue manager at noon. I get out of bed in a rush to get ready. I have less than an hour to make it there on time. And the last thing I need is for him to think that I can't be counted on to be punctual.

Before long, I'm speeding through the streets in my car. Just my luck that the venue is all the way across town. I put the pedal to the metal.

When I finally arrive at my destination, I look at the building in confusion. It's an old warehouse in a rundown district, isolated from other businesses. I guess that the investors must not have gotten to the stage of renovating the building yet. Maybe this area is right at the cusp of some sort of gentrification push?

Getting out of my car, I proceed inside through a door that is already ajar. No bustling crew, no musicians lining up for an audition, no makeshift stage. The building is dusty and dim.

"Hello!" I call out, my voice echoing in the cavernous space. I wonder where I'm expected to perform. Walking around, I scan the old building, looking for I don't know what.

"It's Savannah! We spoke over text." My heels clack loudly against the concrete floor. I must have the wrong address.

I pause, lost. Suddenly, hands grab me from behind.

"Hi Savannah," a man's low, wheezing voice whispers in my ear.

Struggling, I try to turn my head and see who it is, to no avail. His arms are tightly wrapped around me. There's a harsh tang of tobacco and sweat on him. With my arms pinned to my side; I begin to panic.

"Help!" I scream, "Somebody, help!" I thrash about, attempting to knock him off-balance.

Abruptly, a sack is pulled over my head. My nose and mouth are filled with a sickly-sweet smell. My struggles grow weaker.

"I've got you." His voice is the last thing I hear before blackness swallows me.

*　　*　　*

The first thing I realize waking up is the sharp pain. My head pounds as though I'm having the worst hangover ever. My wrists and left ankle feel scraped raw. My hands are cuffed together in front of me, and my left leg is uncomfortably stretched out and chained to a support beam.

The next thing I realize is that I'm lying on an old, dirty mattress. My nose wrinkles at the moldy smell of it. I struggle to roll over, but the chains prevent me from moving freely. Still exhausted from whatever I had been doped with, I simply give up.

The last thing I notice is that my clothes are gone. All except for the red high-heeled shoes. Instead, I'm wearing a crimson sequined evening gown. Stupefied, I recognize it as being eerily similar to one of my stage dresses. I am also wearing some of my favorite pieces of costume jewelry. A ruby necklace, diamond earrings, and a silver comb in my hair. Then it dawns on me that these are all the items that had gone missing in the break-in a few months ago.

And there's something else. I'm no longer wearing panties or a bra. Tears are welling in my eyes. My body and hair feel and smell freshly clean. The scent of an unfamiliar soap wafts up from my skin.

I look around timidly. Nausea overwhelms me at the thought that the guy, whomever he is, must have stripped me naked, washed my body and dressed me in my stolen clothing. Bile is rising rapidly in my throat.

I'm relieved at least to not sense or see any evidence of sexual assault, but I feel deeply violated, nonetheless. Who could have done this to me?

Is he a stalker? A crazed fan who is unable to stop at stealing my belongings and finally had to go so far as to kidnap me?

This room is different from where I was taken, though the layout looks similar. Could be just another side of the building, or somewhere down the block.

A sturdy-looking work light on a tripod stand is placed in the middle of the room. It's directed upwards, spewing out harsh, dull fluorescent light. It bounces off the ceiling and cascades down the surroundings, showcasing countless motes of particles, swirling about haphazardly.

"Help!" I scream. "Someone! ANYONE!"

I must have spent at least half an hour screaming my voice hoarse, but it's hopeless.

Curling up, I continue to whimper as I lie upon the dirty mattress. I hear the distant sounds of rainwater dripping through holes in the roof. Otherwise, everything is still and quiet.

Shivering, I decide to try to get some sleep. I have to conserve my strength to face whatever's coming for me.

*　*　*

I awake to the sound of a car door slamming shut, followed by heavy footsteps outdoors moving toward the building. I tense up.

There's no window in the room I'm in, so I'm not sure what time of day it is. Or how long I had been asleep.

With a creak, the heavy iron door to the room swings open. I flinch, bracing for the worst.

The man who walks in is very tall and slightly overweight.

Besides his size, he seems relatively unassuming, with thin blond hair that's parted in the middle and a plain face. Somehow, he looks familiar. I have seen him before. He had been in the crowd. I remember those eyes. Watching me. Feverishly.

He lumbers forward awkwardly, as though not used to being watched. Stopping several feet away from me, he glances at me tentatively.

"Who are you?" My voice trembles with fear. I watch him warily as he fidgets, carrying two brown paper bags.

"Hello, Savi." He talks in a deep baritone. "That's what your friends call you, right?"

I don't speak for a moment. Helpless rage rises within me.

"You're not my friend." I stare the man down.

He meets my steel gaze with placid blue eyes, then looks down. I sense that he's not the brazen type.

"I'm more than a friend now, Savi." He inches closer. "I'm your new manager." Leaning down cautiously, the "manager" gently sets one of the brown bags down on the concrete floor next to me. Then he quickly retreats. "I'm also a true fan."

"I have a manager. What do you want from me?" I utter. "Just let me go." I'm horrified at the fact that the stalker is making no attempt to hide his face.

"I've always wondered how you hit those really high notes on stage," the kidnapper continues, as though he hadn't heard my plea. His gaze is mostly still fixed on the ground. Every few minutes he looks up at me, then averts his eyes rapidly. "You'll have to demonstrate for me sometime." His tone is civil, like he's just a regular fan at a meet-and-greet session. Somehow, this makes him even more terrifying.

"Please!" I refuse to indulge his demented fantasy. "Please, just don't hurt me. All I want is to go home. I promise I won't tell anyone about you. I promise…" I look at him with desperation in my eyes. Trying to search for some shred of humanity in him. A tear streaks down my face.

"Shhh…" He shushes me as though that would alleviate my fear. I watch cautiously as he crouches down. Hesitantly, he reaches out one thick, meaty finger. I freeze, turning my head away ever so slightly and close my eyes. A finger wipes a salty tear off my cheek. Shuddering, I force open my eyes.

He contemplates the wetness on his finger before popping it into his mouth.

I gag.

He smiles sheepishly. "Your expression…your voice… It reminds me of your singing." He closes his eyes, as though in rapture. "So melancholic and despairing. Like your songs." The man glances at me again, excitement in his eyes. "It awakens something in me!"

I remain silent, shrinking away. Whatever is awakening in this lunatic, I want no part of it.

"Sing something for me," he requests. "How about, 'I'd Rather Go Blind'? It's my personal favorite." With anticipation, he bends his arms and puts his open hands together in front of him.

It's one of my go-tos. I've sung it countless times. But this is madness!

Mute, I shake my head forcefully.

"Please…please…please…" The man begs. "This would mean so much to me."

"No!"

He scowls and pouts. "I *own* you now. You better do what I say!"

"No fucking way!" I yelp. "I'm not some puppet that you can push around and toy with!"

Rage churns inside of me. "You better let me go right this moment, freak!" The last word just slips out of my mouth.

At first, the man keeps still. He is staring at me as though he's unable to comprehend my refusal. Then, his face twists into a rictus of rage. I quake.

Jumping up, he grabs a broken glass-top table that is leaning against the wall. Turning, he flings it against the opposite wall. I scream at the loud crashing noise as the table shatters.

Storming across the room, he begins to seize other objects in the room: chairs, buckets, cleaning equipment. Everything he manages to get a hold of is immediately ravaged in a fit of strength and fury. I fear it's just a matter of time before he gets to me.

"Alright!" I yelp. There's a tightness in my chest. "I'll sing!"

The man stops. His big barrel chest heaves as he glances at me. The room is filled with the sound of his harsh panting. He drops the broom that he broke in two. His twisted mouth gradually transforms into a grin.

He hastens toward a small wooden table in the corner and parks it just in front of the light fixture, whose beam he redirects towards me. Immediately I raise my arms, momentarily blinded by the intense, sudden flood of light.

He also manages to find the last usable chair and parks it down beside the table. Putting down the other brown bag he brought in, the man plops down on the chair. His body is leaning forward, elbows resting on his thighs, hands clasped together under the seat. A child-like grin smears his face.

Feeling his eyes on me, I close mine. I'm still seeing stars from the onslaught of light. This is just too strange. I can't do this.

Bound and chained, I try to center myself. It's an ordinary night. You're onstage. You're ready to perform. The crowd is watching you.

Keeping my eyes shut, I begin. My voice stutters out of my throat. Is it really mine?

Something t-t-told me it was o-o-over
When...when I saw you and h-her talkin'
Something deep d-down in my s-soul said, "Cry, girl"

I continue to sing unsteadily, going in and out of rhythm, mumbling and stammering some words.

This can't get any weirder. I feel like both crying and laughing at the same time. Can't be happening. Some psycho had come to my performances to stalk me, broke into my home, stole my belongings, tricked my agent into setting up a phony audition, kidnapped me, and is now making me give a private performance like some parrot in a cage. Must be a nightmare.

A rustling sound prompts me to open my eyes. The stalker removes a bottle from the brown bag. Then he takes a swig. Looks like beer. I eye it for a moment, wondering if I will get an opportunity to snatch it and knock him over the head.

After a few more gulps, the blond man thumps the half-empty bottle on the table. He stands up and starts to unbuckle his belt.

The next line in the song catches in my throat. I wrap my arms around myself.

"Keep going!" The man barks at me. His brows are furrowed.

He seems like a wild animal on the verge of pouncing.

I follow his order. My voice is a wreck; I stutter badly and strain to hit the notes. I sniffle. Tears stream down my cheeks.

Oooo, I w-w-would rather, I would r-rather go b-b-blind, boy
Th-th-than to see you walk aw-w-way from me, ch-ch-child, no…

I close my eyes again but can't shut out the sound of him unzipping his pants. Panicking, I peek and immediately wish I hadn't. He's holding his veiny erection in one beefy fist. And he has begun to rhythmically tug at it with his eyes trained on me. I gulp in dismay and trepidation. I'd give anything to not witness this obscenity. But the fright of what he may do to me while I'm not looking keeps my eyes peeled.

To my greatest horror, the madman was just starting. From the pocket of his jacket, he pulls out a crumpled ball of black fabric. With shock and disgust, I soon realize that they are my missing bra and panties.

The pervert shoves the undergarments in his face and inhales deeply. A grin of contentment crosses his face as he sniffs. I try to keep singing through the bile that is now in the back of my mouth.

He wraps my intimate things around his member, using the silken fabric to stroke his phallus. While staring at me.

Not being able to bear the sight before me any longer, I shut my eyes tight. I am cringing at the sounds of the blond man pleasuring himself. Please, please, don't let him touch me. I'll do anything.

At this point, I'm no longer singing. Just a bunch of words disgorged out of my mouth. My voice is getting weaker. He doesn't seem to notice.

Soon after, I hear sharp groans. Against my better judgment, I open my eyes. Just in time to see the man come. Body twitching, he sprays all over my undergarments. The white liquid, stark against black silk, drips down over his hand and lands on the concrete floor. With a moan, he slumps back, sated. I barely get the last words out through my clenched lips.

He is still for a moment. Head tilted back, breathing heavily. One hand is still stroking. At a much slower pace than before.

My stomach is heaving.

"Sorry about that," the man sniggers, wiping at his genitals with chagrin, his cheeks reddening. "Guess I got carried away by your beautiful singing."

I pray that he will leave soon, now that he's got what he wanted. There's only so much I can take.

Instead of leaving, the kidnapper begins to straighten up the room. He gathers up the bits of broken furniture from his earlier rage and carries them out of the room. He even fetches a broom and sweeps up the tiny bits of debris that litter the floor.

Through all this, I watch silently. I'm afraid that any word from me, or any sudden movement, may trigger his rage again.

At the moment though, humming blissfully, he seems to be as docile as a baby sloth.

"There." The blond man straightens, dusting his hands off theatrically as he surveys his handiwork. He turns to me with eager eyes, as though searching for some sign of approval. I quickly look away, unable to even feign anything remotely close to what he's expecting.

Fortunately, his response is a mere shrug. He points to the other brown bag on the floor. Cautiously, I pick it up and reach inside.

It's tiny. Feels light and soft. With an acute sense of apprehension, I pull out my hand. There's a small ziplock bag with a smidgen of white powdery substance in it.

"I know how much you like it." He smirks, head slightly cocked. The nutjob is probably waiting for a heartfelt thanks from me. Realizing that he's not getting it, his face darkens. "There's a lot more where that came from. If you behave!"

I should be wary of things that are supplied by him. It could be anything, really. On the other hand, I would say that it's been a rather bad day. And I need all the help I can get.

Not thinking straight, I scramble to open the bag. My shaky hands are bothersome. I tug hard and almost spill the whole contents. Hastily, I shake out everything onto the back of my hand and start snorting like a starved piglet. When it's all gone, I throw my head back. I needed this. More than air to my lungs.

He's treading toward the door now. My spirits lift. The door shuts behind him with a heavy clang. I can hear his feet crunching on the gravel outside. The sound of his car door opening fills me with joy. But that's quickly dashed at the noises of the man slamming the door and walking back.

Within moments, he is back in the room. His arms are laden with packages of chips and pastries, bottled water, another one of my missing evening gowns, and other sundry items. He sets down all these items next to me.

"Here. Anything else?"

Keys for my cuffs would be nice. And a loaded gun please. To blow your head off!

I am incredibly thirsty. I struggle to grab one of the water bottles with my cuffed hands. Fumbling the bottle open, I gulp down the contents.

He just gazes at me, all smiles. Elated by the fact that I obviously like his "gifts." I swipe harshly at my wet mouth, glaring at him. I must look like a lunatic. Tousled hair, chapped lips, rumpled dress, a trace of white powder on my nostrils, bound in chains.

"Take this, too," he says, thrusting a pair of metal buckets toward me. When I don't take them, he gingerly sets them down on the floor next to the other items. One is half-filled with water with a small towel draped over its side.

"For washing up. And...you know." He chuckles. I stare at him, wondering how in the world a man who has the audacity to masturbate in front of a stranger would balk at mentioning bodily functions.

"Don't worry," he continues, stepping closer. He extends one fleshy hand and I freeze. Looking down at my own lap, I try to remain calm as he strokes my tangled hair.

"Everything's going to be fine. I'll take good care of you." He looks fascinated by my hair, rubbing it between his fingers. "Just be a good girl and do as I say. Okay?"

Nothing will ever be okay again. I continue to stare down at my lap, fighting tears, fully aware that the hand that's fondling my hair is the same one as the hand that he utilized for his unspeakable act. Catching a whiff of chlorine and something fishy, I retch.

Eventually, he gets up and leaves. He was kind enough to shift the light back to the ceiling before he left.

When the heavy door slams shut behind him, and the rumble of his car engine fades, I can finally breathe again.

Sinking back onto the dirty mattress, I look up at the water-stained ceiling. And weep myself to sleep.

* * *

A sound wakes me up. I jolt up. Before I can get my bearings, I feel a weight crash down on top of me.

It's him. Wild-eyed, snarling. I scream, but he immediately covers my mouth with his big, hot palm. I'm suffocating under the pressure of him. The smell of alcohol wafts into my nostrils.

"Shut up!" he shouts, shaking me. I struggle to suppress my terrified sobs. To my disbelief, he is crying, tears glistening on his twisted features. He starts moaning, as though he's in pain.

The kidnapper moves the hand that isn't on my mouth. I notice a silver flash. A knife! I thrash about desperately. But it's futile. He brings the knife up to my face.

"I have to do this," he mutters. "Don't you see? There's no other way…"

Pleading with my eyes, I frantically try to shake my head.

"The only way, to make you mine. Mine and mine alone…" The psycho seems to be in a trance, repeating himself over and over. He clutches the handle of the knife so tightly that his knuckles whiten. I'm hyperventilating.

Then he slices the side of my face, near my left eye. I shriek. My scream is muffled by his hand. I feel hot blood trickling down my face. My vision blurs. My breathing turns to quick gasps.

But the worst is yet to come.

The deranged man takes his hand off my mouth to reach into his pocket for something else. I scream at the top of my lungs.

Desperate incoherent wailing. But no one comes.

He pulls out whatever he was searching for. Seeing sparks and flicker of flame, I realize it's a lighter. As I watch in horror, he brings the glinting metal over to the fire, twisting the knife as he heats up the blade.

"There." The blade is so glossy, it almost looks translucent.

Swiftly, he brings it back to my face, hovering just over my left eye. My body goes cold with dread. I struggle mightily to free myself of his grip, but he gets me pinned down good. Raw panic is in my shrieks.

Nervously, he squashes the blade down onto my closed lid, piercing the skin with searing metal.

Darkness swallows me whole.

*   *   *

I come to unbearable agony. The searing pain triggers me to howl despairingly.

Something is wrong. The room is darker. And spinning. Then it hits me. Can't see out of my left eye. I raise my hand to touch it. It's covered with some cloth. The bastard must have dressed my wound. My body is quavering. I hug myself, lying in a fetal position.

"Got something for the pain." I flinch at the sound of his voice. I cower, desiring to bury myself in the mattress. Away from *him*.

"Here." Something lands on the mattress, close to my arms. I peek out of my right eye. A small, fat ziplock bag. I look up at him. He nods. With elbow pressing on the mattress, I prop my upper body up to the side. I swoop up the bag and tear it open. With one hooked finger, dredging up as much powder as possible, I bring it up to my nose. And inhale.

My tongue feels numb, nose burning. Somehow, I can see through the faux-tin ceiling tiles. I gaze at the moonlit, smoky night sky.

Now I'm floating through the restless, crimson clouds. I sway my limbs effortlessly.

Out of the blue, I'm tearing through the stratosphere. Atop a majestic eagle. The softness of its feathers caresses my palms.

Noises crash me back down to earth. I see flashes of him getting up. Leaving me to writhe, broken, upon the mattress. Sounds of him opening the door. And the muttering right before he leaves.

"I'm sorry. Had to do it. No other man will want you now. But I do. I'll take good care of you. Forever."

The last thing I remember before passing out is the clang of the door shutting. With grim finality.

*   *   *

The next morning, I don't react or move as he comes into the room. I just lay there on the dirty mattress. Drained of energy and wracked with pain. Whatever comes next, I'm unable to muster the will to care. At this point, death would be a mercy.

Outside, he pauses for several seconds before opening the door. Then he plods into the room, eyes glued to the floor.

Lying there, half-blind and delirious, I feel hysterical laughter bubbling up inside me. He acts like a misbehaved student who's been summoned to the principal's office.

He creeps closer, then slowly looks up. I still haven't moved.

"Sorry." I glance up. Above me, he is holding out a bouquet of red roses. His face is expectant, not directly looking at my eyes.

"For you." I stay still. Just staring, the good eye watering, the damaged eye nothing but a crater of pain in my face. Fury throbs in me, coalescing with the beating of my heart.

After a while, he begins to look crestfallen. He fills the silence with mumbling.

"I really had no choice. I did it for us." He shuffles bashfully in place.

Jolting up with strength I didn't know I had, I snatch the roses away from him with my cuffed hands. Shrieking, I tear them to pieces.

A flurry of petals rains down upon the mattress. Shredding the bouquet, I hardly notice the thorns cutting my hands. It's almost a relief, in comparison to the throbbing pain coming from the wound in my left eye.

"There's NEVER gonna be an 'us'!" I scream and sob. "I'd rather die than have anything to do with you!"

I rip the bandage off my face, shoving my face forward. For him to see. He grimaces and looks away. This monster can't even bear the sight of the atrocity of his own making.

Continuing to holler, I strain forward, attempting to scratch and kick at him, despite the restraints that are gnawing into my skin.

"Psycho! You piece of shit! I hate you! HATE YOU!"

My whole body is pulsating with wrath. Shoulders stooped, grimacing, he steps backwards every time my talon-like fingers get close to him.

"You'll change your mind," he states matter-of-factly. "One

day you'll realize that I'm right." He pulls out a little pill and throws it on the mattress. "Here. For the pain."

Despite my profound hatred of him, I scrabble for the tiny object, secretly praying for relief. I return my glare at him.

"Please don't look at me like that," he pleads. "Look, I brought more food."

I don't even look at the bag of fast food that hits the concrete floor beside me. I just continue to glare, body erect, desperate for the pain pill to kick in.

"Oh! I almost forgot." He rushes eagerly out of the room, and I hear the sound of heavy dragging through the doorway.

"Here. I'll prop it right against the wall over here."

Staring without blinking, I watch him lean a tall mirror against the far wall. Seeing my reflection in it, I almost throw up. My hair is wild and greasy, skin paper-white. The red dress I'm wearing is ripped, exposing one shoulder. Half of my face is mutilated. Left eye is swollen shut, mangled skin for an eyelid, the slice on my cheek scabs over. I look almost as horrendous as I feel.

"I wanted to make sure you feel comfortable. This place is your stage now. Home." I almost implode at the mention of the last word. The delusional lunatic grins. "No one knows where you are. We're safe."

Silent, I observe as he takes out a little medical kit and tosses it towards me.

"I cauterized your wound so it wouldn't get infected, but just in case, there are some bandages and antibiotic ointment in there."

I stay still. My mind is consumed with thoughts. Can't go on living like this. I refuse. I immensely regret not going through with my suicide attempt just a few days before the kidnapping.

Could have been lying underground by now, lifeless. Forgotten and at peace.

If only.

I consider banging my head against the beam my leg is chained to. Or refusing medical care, letting my wounds fester. But I quickly dismiss the ideas. Too slow, and there's no guarantee either would actually kill me. The last thing I want, should I fail, is for him to keep me alive. Maimed, and possibly brain-damaged. Must find something quicker. And surer.

While I'm ruminating, I barely notice my kidnapper leave. He mumbles something and drops another ziplock bag, but I'm lost in my dark thoughts, obsessed with finding a way out.

Out of his grasp, or out of this life.

* * *

Sometime in the night, a draft of cold air disrupts my agitated sleep. I shiver. Stumbling to my feet, I try to move the mattress. Could be a hole in the ceiling, or a crack on the wall. If I shift position, I might just avoid the chilly gusts.

As I struggle to move the heavy mattress, something sharp grazes my foot. I jump, looking down. I make out something brown and shiny on the floor. Hand trembling, I reach down, gingerly picking it up.

It's a long, thin shard of glass.

* * *

God exists. That's the only explanation for this little miracle.

Something up there heard my prayer and elected to liberate me.

Can't sleep. Been tossing and turning for some time now. Spent body, sapped spirit. But my mind is vigilant as ever.

That piece of glass…it must be from the bottle that maniac had smashed against the wall. When it shattered, a shard must have ended up concealed beneath a corner of the mattress.

I spring up, sitting bolt upright. Now is as good a time as any. Promptly, I reach under the mattress and draw out the shard. It glints in my hand. A fragment of my profile is reflected in its smooth, pellucid surface. The eye of a desperado.

I hold the piece of glass against my throat with both hands. They are shaking. I feel wetness in my eyes. I gulp hard.

I lower my hands.

I could easily slit my wrists or throat right then and there. And my suffering would be over.

But then…why do I feel so unresolved? Here is my salvation, right in my hand. I have the power to prevent that monster from ever touching me again.

Is it vengeance that I seek? Perhaps it's best to save the shard for his jugular. Or his eye. An eye for an eye. But at the thought of that, I know that isn't it. Can't risk failing and having him snag this piece of glass from me. My only salvation.

Maybe a different sort of revenge, then. Perhaps I ache for the stalker to be an audience to my suicide. A show he wouldn't be jacking off to. A front-row seat to the demise of his little broken canary.

But I quickly dismiss that too. I don't need an audience. I've had more than enough of enduring that slimy creep's eyes on me. Besides, I might lose courage at a critical moment. And then what?

Why, then? For some unfathomable reason, I'm not able to take the out I was dying for. The escape I would have been eager to sell my soul to the devil for not fifteen minutes ago. I'm missing something.

I grip the glass so tightly in my hand that it cuts into my flesh, causing me to bleed. But still, I don't let go.

Could it be…that deep inside my heart, I want to live?

But why?

Certainly not the white powder I've grown to love too much and depend on.

Definitely not the crazy exes that used me as a punching bag, physically and mentally.

No offspring to care for, no significant other to pour your heart into and no known relatives.

I have absolutely nothing worth fighting for. And no one to mourn me when I'm dead. So why? WHY?!

I do cherish beholding the ever-changing, eloquent sunset from my apartment window. The fiery hues of orange, pink, and violet in the sky, concocting a symphony of ravishing mayhem while the tart taste of wine tingles my taste buds.

I do relish dipping my legs in that stream which runs through the park. Can almost feel the cool water slipping around my calves. The soothing touch of the breeze caressing my face.

And I do worship those brief moments before a performance. When the lights turn down low and the audience goes perfectly silent and still. Seems like everything is suspended in time. Except for the gentle wheeze of my breathing and the thrumming beat of my heart.

In those significantly evocative seconds, under the spotlight, in my mind's eye, I'm standing on the surface of a star. Bursting with an exuberance of passion, vitality and hope. Ready to broadcast the euphonious tales out to the humbling, eternal universe.

Suddenly, Leon's face materializes in my mind's eye. I can even hear his words.

You're the strongest woman I've ever met.

I wish you could hear yourself the way I hear you.

I believe in you, Savi.

Tears sting the corners of my eyes.

Leon.

I never had the chance to really express how much he means to me. If there is still something in life I can't help but cling to, Leon is, without a shadow of a doubt, a significant part of it.

I can see his face clearly, as though he is standing before me. Smiling at me. His gentle eyes fill my heart with tranquility and warmth.

I love him.

This assertion astounds me. As if it arose out of someone else.

But it's not wrong. I do. Don't I? The feeling is unmistakable. It's been there all along, lurking underneath the surface.

No man has ever cared for me like he does. No person has ever showed adoration for me like he has.

No one has ever made my heart flutter and my head spin with so many possibilities and so much hope that it hurts the way he does.

Is that a definition of love? Has to be. What else is capable of hurting so beautifully in this absurd world? I may never know.

I'm weeping now, accidentally smearing my face with blood as I reach up to wipe tears away. I'm past caring, allowing the coppery taste of it to ground me.

Does Leon feel the same way?

Would he still believe in me if he could see me now?

A one-eyed, scarred chanteuse. Preaching the blues.

I snort derisively, disgusted with myself.

Was Leon right? I sob harder. Snot and tears integrate with blood, pollocking my visage.

Do I just need to give myself permission to be happy? To live?

I open my hand and look down at the shard perching on my grazed palm.

A stray, wounded songbird.

Should I cease its pain, sorrow, and existence once and for all?

Or does it merit another day, among the living? To heal?

*   *   *

I sleep for several hours before I am woken by the sound of my kidnapper returning. He looks disheveled. It's only fair that I wasn't the only one without a good night's sleep.

I can tell he is wary of my mood; he moves slowly, as if afraid that I'll fly off the handle. But after he looks at me, his face relaxes. Whatever he sees seems to assuage his worries.

"Look like you're in better spirits." He edges closer. Suppose he notices the fresh dressing on my now-defunct eye, my straightened posture, and the calm on my face. I keep quiet.

"Would you please sing again for me?" He's practically on his knees. "Please, I'm dying to hear that song again. From you."

I nod lightly.

He grins. Without hesitation, he starts to unbuckle the belt, dropping his trousers and underwear to his ankles and takes his seat as before. He takes my bra and panties out of his pocket and puts them on the table. Can't tell if he washed them. A cynical chuckle escapes my lips.

And they say chivalry is dead.

He looks up expectantly. "Is this alright?" My eyes narrow. *Why wouldn't it be? Would you like a beer and some popcorn too?* I think bitterly.

"What if I say no?" I scoff.

He glares at me. With his pants still down, he gets up, comically shuffles his feet a little towards me, his penis dangling from side to side. "I could easily blind the other eye, if you so wish!" he exclaims. Venom in his voice.

"Okay, I'll do it!" I struggle to my feet, smoothing over my scruffy dress.

Relief washes over his face. He shuffles backwards to return to his seat.

Taking several deep breaths and trying to see through him, I clear my throat.

And I begin.

Oooo, so you see, I love you so much
That I don't wanna watch you leave me, baby
Most of all, I just don't, I just don't wanna be free, no…

I marvel at myself, wondering where this voice is coming from. As if the pain and the fear had gone. Instead, I'm fueled with something foreign, yet familiar. Vibrant and tenacious.

He looks ill. Sitting still, slack-jawed, arms hanging by his side.

His flaccid prick forgotten.

Than to see you walk away, see you walk away from me, yeah
Whoo, baby, baby, baby, I'd rather be blind…

Finishing with a flourish, I take a bow.

The man continues to be still for several moments. His mouth is slightly ajar. I regard him closely, breathing hard from the exertion my performance required.

Snapping out of it, he lurches up and quickly pulls up and buckles his pants. Then he starts to enthusiastically clap his hands, obviously delighted with the rendition of his favorite song.

"Bravo!" he shouts, applauding furiously. "Bravo!" He wipes a tear from his eye. "You put some soul into that. It's as if the words come from your very own heart. Thank you."

I offer him a reluctant smile.

He begins to amble towards the door.

"Well done, Savi. I'm gonna get you more supplies and you know…" He smirks and clumsily mimics a snorting act with his hand. "Let me know if you need anything. You deserve it."

My heart skips a beat.

"You know…" I say, trying to sound as even-toned as possible, "since I've done such a good job, I wonder if I could ask you for a little favor?" I try mightily to tame the flame of emotions that's burning a hole in my gut.

He turns around, hands on hips. "What is it?" the man queries cautiously.

"Well," I utter, "my ankle is getting really sore. I think this manacle is cutting off my circulation. Could you please un-cuff my leg and let me walk around the room for just a few minutes?" I beam.

He glares at me. "No, sorry," he mumbles. Suddenly, I'm suffocating.

"Please! You can keep my hands cuffed, obviously. We don't want a blood clot, do we? Next thing I will have to be amputated. Without a leg, I can't stand on my own two feet. Air circulation and body mass will be affected. I will not be able to sing as well. That is, indeed, very bad news!" My heart is in my throat. "For both of us," I swiftly add.

He seems to ponder this for a moment. Then he reaches into his pocket, takes out a key, and tosses it close to my feet.

"Just a few minutes. Don't do anything stupid. Or else..." he threatens, while tapping his right eye.

I thank him profusely, trying not to let my fingers shake as I bend over and seize the key. The slight heft of the small piece of metal feels unreal. I slip the key into the hole on the manacle. I twist and jerk my hand, pretending to be struggling to turn it.

"I can't...quite..." With a grunt, I let the little key slip out of my grasp and fall to the floor. "Are you sure this is the right key? Doesn't seem to work."

"It's right," he insists. "Try again."

I pick up the key and attempt once more to turn it in the lock. But again, it slips from my grasp.

"It's not working," I complain, slumping my shoulders. At the same time, my hand creeps down under the mattress. My jittery fingers feel around the area.

Nothing. It's gone! A cold sweat runs down the length of my spine. I quickly move my hand up and down.

A finger brushes against a cold, brittle object. I breathe a huge sigh of relief internally.

"What in hell," he blurts, impatience thick in his voice. "Let me try." I remain perfectly still as he nears me.

He's almost within reach now. The little piece of glass pressed against the palm of my clenched hand.

I wait. At the ready. Sounds like I'm holding my heart to my ear. It's deafening. Is he not hearing this?

He kneels beside me on one knee. I observe the thinning hair at the top of his blond head as he bends over, reaching for the key on the floor.

He looks up sharply as I'm about to make my move. I smile. But my body tenses, wondering if he suspects something. He scans my eyes, then picks up the key.

Casually, I extend my leg toward him, proffering my ankle for easy reach.

He drifts even closer. Tangy sweat and sandalwood scent flitter up my nostrils.

I tighten my grip on the shard of glass.

Holding my breath, I watch as the man bends down.

Slipping the little key into the manacle.

Turning it effortlessly…

His head shoots up. A look of confusion suffuses his face.

Then alarm.

The shard is reflected in his widening eyes.

Like a vulture, swooping down the valley of death.

THE DESCENT

There is nothing sweeter than the sound of applause when the wheels hit the tarmac after a turbulent flight.

From the cockpit, I receive their gratitude, a gentle rumble of thunder. It's stupid, I know, a pointless habit of the upper middle class, who only get to fly a handful of times in their sorry lives. I hear it at least once a day, sometimes twice, and it never gets old. I revel in it for a moment as we pull into the gate.

"Another day, another horrifying crash narrowly avoided," I mumble to myself, my breath soaked in whiskey. Late-night layovers always suck ass, but I try to liven it up a bit whenever I get the opportunity. I could fly this thing with my eyes closed, and everyone knows it—especially my co-pilot Brendan, who says nothing in return.

Jealousy's a hell of a drug. I think that's why he never really took a liking to me.

Michelle's voice comes over the PA, welcoming everyone to this shithole in the middle of nowhere, telling everyone to stay seated till the seatbelt light turns off. She signs off with her signature giggle, a laugh that might have been cute when she was younger, but I've heard it so many goddamn times it sounds like a woodpecker digging into my brain.

Alice walks into the cockpit to bring me one last drink before we deplane. This is only her third or fourth flight, but she already knows my order—Jack with a splash of Coke to wash it down. Her mixing skills are impeccable. She's a sweet little thing, a twenty-something redhead with hips that sway in such a way I can't take my eyes off them. I don't think she wants me to, either. She's been making eyes at me for as long as she's been here, and who am I to deny her? I only aim to please.

As we walk through the gate, over the shitty carpeting that hasn't been changed since the 90s, Alice decides to make some conversation.

"That was some storm, wouldn't you say?" Alice says, deliberately pushing her hair to the side.

Michelle rolls her eyes, thinking no one's going to notice. I do. I notice everything. Even the way Brendan stares at Alice's ass as she walks. It's incredibly rude of him. She is not some piece of meat to be objectified, Brendan!

"When you've been doing this as long as I have," I say, readjusting my duffel over my shoulder, crossing over to the other side of Alice, blocking Brendan's line of sight as I do so. "You learn to lean into the turbulence. It's all about surrendering to the storm, not trying to fight against it."

Alice ogles me as we get onto the people mover. I walk along it, enjoying the feeling of brushing past the world at double speed. In the corner of my eye, I catch my reflection in the glass windows of a duty-free store with its lights shut off. I grin.

It's barely a five-minute walk across this airport in this small city God forgot, and we head straight for the check-in counter of an airport hotel.

"So, we check in, and head straight for the bar?" Michelle asks.

"Yeah, I could use a beer, or five," Brendan says. I think he has a drinking problem. I tried to talk to him about it once, while we were a couple thousand feet above ground, but he didn't respond. He's not one for talking.

A few of the other attendants agree, including Alice.

"Sounds like a plan," I say, though I have no intention of doing that. I have other plans for this evening.

Michelle's the first to check in, then Brendan, and the rest of us line up behind them. I'm at the back of the queue, right behind Alice. It takes everything in my power not to run my hands over the curves that so pleasantly fill out her stewardess uniform. I lean forward, inches away from her perfect brunette waves.

"There's nothing I want more than to make you pant and whimper like a bitch in heat while I fuck you silly," I whisper, only loud enough for her to hear, my hot breath pushing against her hair. Goosebumps form along her neck.

She jumps a little, and sneaks a look back at me, her pink lips gaped wide open in shock. I know this game. A pilot and a stewardess, so cliche. This is a bad thing we're doing. She can't seem too eager. It makes it less fun for both of us.

I flash her a smile that would set a murderer free, so innocent, so sincere. It's almost like I never said anything.

For a few seconds she stares at me, aghast, before she blushes and turns back around. She leans her head back a bit, her hair falling from her shoulders. Stepping up, she checks in and stands to the side, pretending to look for something in her purse.

The last one on the line, I grab my room keys—they always

give you two, just in case. I walk past her, and off-handedly drop one of them into her purse. She pretends not to notice, but a smile tugs at her lips.

*   *   *

I get into the room, and the stench of stale cigarette smoke hits me in the face like a ton of bricks. Really sets a mood. I toss my duffel bag into the corner and open a window, letting the cool night air into the room. That's the only good thing about places like this, the fresh coastal air.

God I can't wait to get back to the city.

I toss my hat and my watch onto the small wooden desk in the corner of the room. The minibar is woefully understocked, but it'll have to do also. I grab a nip of scotch and throw it back in one gulp. A familiar burn runs down the back of my throat. Tossing the empty bottle onto the table, I reach for my wallet, looking to see if I remembered to stash any condoms. Gotta be safe; God knows I'm not trying to have some little shit running around. Alice didn't seem like the pro-life kind, but you can never be too sure. Being a stewardess is a popular profession for psychos.

None in there. I check my duffel bag, opening every zipper and secret compartment I can find. Maybe past Chris did me a solid. He did, the beautiful bastard. I find a crumpled pack of Trojans, old as sin. Gotta be expired, but it's better than nothing.

Win some, lose some. I shrugged. Expiration dates are bullshit anyway.

Carefully, I undo my watch, and tuck that into the duffel on my way to the bathroom. Gotta freshen up a bit before Alice comes.

I take a quick shower. The cold water feels good on my face, jolting me awake. Over my head, the bathroom light buzzes, as if at any moment it might burst into a shower of sparks and glass. The faucet creaks as I turn it off.

Stepping out, I pat myself down with their complimentary towel, and it feels like I'm rubbing sandpaper against my skin. Hanging up the towel, I look at the wall-length mirror that every shitty motel seems to have. My reflection stares back at me. Empty eyes hide behind a smile so perfected that no one but me could tell it was forced.

And then I remember Alice is coming, and it turns real again—for a second.

"You still got it," my reflection says back to me.

The shower behind me isn't big enough for two people, so we'll just have to make do with the twin bed that a thousand other people have fucked on, maybe the chair in the corner too, though it's in dire need of reupholstering. I've done it in worse places, if I'm being honest.

I lay down on the bed, arms crossed behind my head, air drying save for a corner of the bed sheet covering my crotch. I don't have any time to waste. They're gonna be expecting us at the bar, and I don't want to hear another tirade from Michelle about workplace etiquette. I'm just trying to feel good, is that such a crime? Isn't that what everyone's trying to do?

A minute passes. Then two.

I grab the remote and turn on the TV to one of the seven channels they get in this backwoods part of the country. The Rockets game is on. I never really cared much about sports, but it's better than sitting here ass naked in silence. I tap my fingers against the remote, just to give my mind something to do.

Where the fuck is she? I think, just as the lock clicks and the door creaks open.

Alice steps in, a vision in a tight blue dress that I can't wait to tear off her. She looks at me, surprised but unable to turn away.

"Someone's in a hurry," she giggles.

That's what Michelle's giggle probably sounded like twenty years ago.

"What about the others? They're probably waiting downstairs."

"I don't give a shit."

"But they'll get suspicious, us both not being there."

"Stop your yakking and put that mouth to good use, young lady. Before I strangle somebody!" I rip the sheet that's barely concealing my engorged twizzler.

*   *   *

The next day I'm back in the greatest city in the world. It was an early flight. Still feeling hungover and sore, I let Brendan take charge this go-round. Alice tries to get my attention as we are walking out of the terminal, but I ignore her. Can't have her thinking the night before was something it wasn't.

It's a cold day; the sky, the streets, the buildings, the whole goddamn city is just different shades of grey. The clouds gathered overhead threaten to open up at any moment. It feels like home.

I pick up a cup of coffee, black, from a café at the subway stop by the airport. The punk girl with the pink hair and piercings is there, and she welcomes me home. They're freaks, but punks are always nicer than people give them credit for.

You gotta be when you tell society where it can shove its expectations. To each their own, I guess.

I stop by Sal's newspaper stand to catch up on what bullshit I've missed back at home while gallivanting around the world. I pick up a copy of the *Times* and the *Post*; I like to see all perspectives. If you don't, you just end up another brainwashed zombie walking around, parroting bullshit and waiting for the sweet embrace of death. I got shit to do before then.

As I'm handing Sal cash, I spot a familiar face walking down the sidewalk. That crooked nose, angular jawline. That high forehead. Could it be? Nah, it couldn't, Brad moved out of the city years ago. But lo and behold, it is—my old college buddy.

Brad and I were inseparable during college. We pledged into our frat, Kappa Alpha Omega, the same semester. Even if we hadn't seen each other in years, we'd always be brothers. There's something special about the bond that's made when you struggle and triumph together, having each other's back, covered in dirt and vomit together, drinking shot after shot of whiskey till you can't even see straight. If I thought *I* was wild, Brad was twice that.

There was a day—maybe our sophomore year—that I'll never forget. We were lying around in our frat house. The floor was covered in empty beer cans, crumpled papers, dust, and stubs. Taking one last hit of a joint, Brad stumbled off the couch towards the fridge looking for another beer. It was empty.

I shrugged, thinking that was a sign to call it for the night, but no, Brad had something else in mind. Our frat house was two houses down from his ex's sorority house, and they were preparing for the homecoming party—which meant they were *stacked* with booze. And Brad decided that we were gonna take some of it.

They won't even notice, he said.

His plan was to waltz in there and cause a scene with his ex. He'd start yelling and causing a big distraction, big enough that they wouldn't even notice me sneaking in through the side door and snagging one of the kegs they'd bought. It was foolproof, he'd said.

Well, everything did go according to plan, for the most part. He'd stormed their house like the fucking Bastille, drawing their attention while I pulled off the heist. I did so—flawlessly, I might add. But Brad didn't end up coming back to the house that night. I passed out on the couch waiting for him.

The next morning, he stumbled into the house, hungover as hell. When I asked him where he'd been all night, he proudly told me about the *epic* threesome he had with his ex and one of her sorority sisters. I didn't believe him at first, before he showed me a couple of hickeys on his neck, and I stopped him before he started to strip right then and there to prove it to me. Maybe he exaggerated a bit about the details, but as far as I'm concerned, Brad was everything I aspired to be.

He looks almost exactly like I remember him, except for a couple of extra pounds and a shorter haircut that must be from some mediocre barbershop. He's wearing a coat one size over, wrinkled jeans and slightly worn running shoes. I wouldn't want to be seen with him in a bar picking up chicks, not that I need to.

Damn, how the mighty had fallen.

I tell Sal to keep the change and I call out to Brad.

He turns around, eyes wide, and makes his way over. "Chris! It's you! How you been, man?" Brad grins.

We do our old fraternity handshake, and I ask him, "What

the hell are you doing here? Couldn't resist the sleaze of the big city for long?"

"Back in town for a couple weeks for business," he says with a laugh. "What have you been up to since college?"

I tell him I'm a pilot, just coming home from a flight. "Aside from that," I say. "Not much has changed. A couple more grey hairs, still horny as fuck, you know how it is."

"That's incredible," he says, more genuine than I think he'd ever been in college. "I'm really happy you're doing something you love. Bet it gets lonely out there though."

I shrug. "You find company. Tarts with tight buns and skirts." I wink.

"It's so important to find your purpose in life," Brad mutters, not really listening to my response. "Lord knows I needed it."

I nod politely and start noticing things I didn't before. The smile on his face is more generous, the light behind his eyes brighter. Something's different about him, I just can't put my finger on it.

"Yeah, a lot has changed since college," Brad goes on to say. "Ever since my wife and I had our two little girls, I've really started to appreciate the little things in life. Not just girls and booze, you know?"

I smile, hiding a feeling I can't quite place.

Brad doesn't seem to notice. "I started volunteering, getting more involved in the community. Just embracing—"

I cut him off. "Hey, it's been real nice catching up with you, B. I hate to cut the conversation short, but my girlfriend and the dog are waiting for me back at the apartment. You know how it is."

Brad slaps me on the shoulder and gives me a laugh that I can only describe as belonging to a dad. "I hear you. Look I'd love to have dinner with you and the missus before I skip town again." He takes out a business card from a pocket inside his coat. "Text me so I have your information, I'd love to catch up." He flashes a smile that cuts through me.

We part ways, and as I'm walking home, I take out his business card. Life Mission Insurance. I toss it in the trash.

It starts to rain. People all around me frantically rush to find cover or pull out an umbrella, but I don't really mind. I'm not a bitch who's afraid of a little water.

My unexpected reunion with Brad plays over and over in my head. I can't stop thinking about that look in his eyes, that pure domesticity that had torn out every fragment of the animal I knew back in school.

Even in college, Brad was a braggart. He told these exaggerated stories just to get in all the sorority girls' pants. He probably hasn't changed at all. There's nothing special about his life. He's just like every other Soulless White Picket Fence American Dream family guy.

If anything, Brad should be jealous of *me*. I've got a great gig. I make good money. I have no nagging wife or hollering kids to go back to. I get to see the world and sleep with beautiful women, often at the same time. I've got more than I can handle for my purpose in life.

My reflection stares back at me from a puddle on the cracked sidewalk.

So why did I lie to Brad? I don't have a dog, let alone a girlfriend. Which is the way I prefer it. Nothing to tie me down, no one to feel guilty about cheating on when I screw my way across the globe.

The question pings around my skull again. *So why lie?*

Maybe there's something else, something I won't even realize I'm missing until I have it. What did Brad call it? My "true path," or whatever. Do I even want to know?

Maybe I am getting a little old for all this bullshit.

All these thoughts crowd my mind, as densely packed as the subway station where I wait for the train to bring me home. I'm sitting on a bench next to a homeless guy who keeps talking to no one but the air around him. My eyes are glued to the newspaper, but I don't read a damn word.

Something wet touches my leg.

I look up to see an old man muttering an apology. In his hand is a folded-up umbrella, dripping wet, that he's using to hold himself up like a makeshift cane. His skin hangs off his body like it's begging to be released, and his eyes are the kind of dark that only comes after decades of living paycheck to paycheck in this city. I see it all the time.

Standing up, I motion with the newspaper to the now-vacant seat. The old man eagerly accepts. I walk over to a gap in the crowd by the track and start to read again. Nothing too interesting. Something about the civil war in the East, some shooting over in Borden. I start to flip the page over to the sports section, when a scream rips through the subway station, echoing over onto itself a thousand times.

On my left, a crowd is huddled around the scream's origin. With their backs turned to me, I can't see much. They're stiff and unmoving, statues frozen in place. Unable to suppress my curiosity, I tuck my newspaper under my arm and make my way over.

As I approach, I can see the faces of the crowd are all horrified, their eyes all fixated on a singular point beyond the platform. Gasps and mutters run their way through as more and more people realize what's going on.

An older woman in a bright green jacket, with brittle, white hair, collapsed in between the tracks, slumped over on her side with her eyes closed. She's only a few inches away from the third rail. She's lucky. A little bit over and she would've fried. A small dog with an orange vest that says *Service Dog* in big white letters is next to her, licking her face trying to wake her up. It doesn't seem to be doing anything.

This big guy, with tattoo-covered arms the size of tree trunks pushes me aside and starts asking people what happened. A young woman steps forward, shaking so badly she can barely speak.

"The lady and her dog were standing next to me," she says, gasping through words. "She seemed kind of sick, breathing really weirdly and stuff. I wanted to ask her if she was alright, but I didn't think it was appropriate, and I had a really long day at—"

"How did she fall?" the man asks, cutting off her terrified babble.

"I don't know," the woman says, on the verge of tears. "One second she was standing up, the next she collapsed on the ground and rolled on the platform, pulling the dog down with her. It all happened so fast; I couldn't even try to stop it."

The man nods his head. "Alright everyone, please move away from the edge."

Without questioning, everyone in the crowd, including me, steps back. The man kneels on the edge of the platform, assessing the situation. Though on the surface he seems to have the situation under control, his muscles are tense, and his eyes are darting everywhere. He's terrified.

He repositions his body and throws his legs over the edge. Just as he's about to lower himself down, the roaring sound of a horn erupts and a dim but rapidly brightening light emits from down the tunnel.

The man freezes mid-motion. He stares down the tunnel, like a deer in headlights. Glancing back, he looks around at the gathered crowd, hoping someone will decide for him. People keep looking at him. Then to the tunnel. Then back.

No one's moving.

He makes eye contact with me, and something inside me leaps into action. I drop everything I'm holding. I run forward, throwing off my coat to a bystander. I jump from the edge of the platform, and land on the tracks with a thud.

The ground shakes beneath my feet, the vibrations getting stronger with each passing second. The dull rumble of the train is growing into a scream that overcomes every fiber of my being.

I sprint over to the woman's still unmoving body. Careful not to move her onto the tracks, I flip her over. With strength I didn't realize I had, I haul her frail body over my shoulders and carry her toward the man, who's still frozen on the lip of the platform. Thankfully, he breaks from his trance. He grabs her from me and lays her down on the ground.

I put my shaking hands on the edge, about to pull myself up. A storm of shouts halts me, and I look up to the crowd who are pointing back at the tracks. I turn around.

The dog.

It's standing between the rails, whimpering and shaking so hard it's nearly vibrating. Slowly, I walk over to it, careful not to scare it any more than it already is. I crouch down, extending my hand, trying my best to keep it from shaking. Whistling, I try to coax the dog over to me.

The dog moves two steps forward, and I inch closer. One of its paws brushes against the quaking track, and it recedes again. The ground is trembling, and it feels like the earth is about to split and consume us both. The light from the head of the train bursts from the tunnel, and the horn fills the air.

With no more time to waste, I stand up and dash across the tracks. I scoop the dog in one arm, grabbing it by its collar to make sure it doesn't jump away. Part of me wants to look to the side, to figure out how much time I have before the inevitable death, but the floodlights make everything bright white.

I sprint back to the side of the tracks, and desperately try to claw up to the platform with one hand. My feet can't find purchase. They keep slipping as the train gets closer.

Hands pull at my shirt and yank me up. I hold my breath. I shut my eyes. A rush of air violently pushes past me. I'm engulfed in the train's storm.

Time slows to a stop.

The only sound is the scream of the train.

Everything is white.

After what seems like an eternity, I slowly open one eye. Then the other.

Inches from my face is a wall of thick, cold steel, shining my reflection back at me. I'm still clutching the dog in my arms, a little too tightly. Releasing my grip, the dog pushes against my chest and leaps to the old woman, who is still unconscious. The man is next to her, seemingly on the verge of tears.

Slowly getting to my feet, I look around at the crowd.

They're all wearing the same look of disbelief. I try to find the person with my jacket. It's the young woman. Wordlessly, she hands it back to me.

For a moment, everybody is quiet.

Then, the homeless guy on the bench stands up and shouts, "You fucking did it!"

The crowd erupts into cheers, applause, and prayers. It sounds sweeter than any landing I've ever done in my life. My blood pounds in my ears and I can't help but have this massive grin plastered on my face. I soak it all in. I feel like a hero. Bloody hell, I *am* one.

Muscle Guy comes over to me and locks me in a massive bear hug. I resist for a second, before collapsing into it and hugging him back.

The train doors open, and people start pouring out. I could only imagine how confused they must be.

*   *   *

When I get off the train, I'm still in a state of shock. The entire walk home, I'm floating on air. The rain feels great against my skin, each droplet sending wave after wave of pure existential ecstasy through my veins.

Life is beautiful. The trees that line the streets near my apartment are greener than they've ever been before. There's a man who's standing outside a bodega near my apartment asking people for change, and I hand him twenty bucks.

"Are you sure?" he asks, looking at the bill like it was radioactive.

"I've never been surer about anything in my entire life," I say, patting him on the shoulder as I keep walking down the road.

I get to my apartment, and I look at everything in there in a new light. All the things I've collected over the years from all the places I've gone now hold memories and experiences I'm grateful for, rather than just being reminders of the shit I'm not doing right now.

I straighten up the apartment, picking up the clothes I left lying around before I left. I open up a window and listen to the sweet rhythm of the rain pounding against the concrete.

I crash down on the couch, my head still buzzing. The image of the old woman sticks out in my mind, and suddenly, I feel the urge to talk to my mom. We haven't had a real conversation in years, not since my dad died. I'm always flying for the holidays and keep promising that I'll get around to seeing her but never do.

I pick up my phone to call her but get distracted when I see a string of unanswered texts from Alice.

Alice: Hey I had a lot of fun last night <3

Alice: I was wondering if you might want to go out for drinks sometime, just you and me?

Alice: Did I do something wrong?

I sigh, realizing just how much of an asshole I'd been, completely ignoring her this morning. She's a good person, and doesn't deserve the cold, silent treatment. Well, there's still time to make it up.

Me: Sorry, you didn't do anything wrong. I had a really bad hangover this morning. I had fun too. I'd love to get drinks sometime. Maybe tomorrow night?

My finger hovers over the drafted text, unsure if I really want to make the leap. My heart pounds in my chest as I press "send."

My phone buzzes in my pocket, and I check it quicker than I've ever checked any message before in my life.

Alice: I totally get it! We drank a lot last night ;) Tomorrow night works for me!

I click the phone off. The screen goes black, and I see my reflection looking back up at me from the darkness. A genuine smile. I almost forgot what it looks like.

*   *   *

The next morning, realizing I got sidetracked by Alice, I pick up the phone to call my mom. As I scroll through my phone, I see the last time she called me was a few years back. Around the time when my dad had died. My old man and I never really got along. We were always butting heads about every little thing. I was never good enough for him, and he was never good enough for me. When I dropped out of my last semester of college to go to flight school, my dad all but disowned me. He told me I wasted his money drinking away the last four years. He wasn't entirely wrong about that, but I'd be damned if I let him know that.

The entire time we were screaming in the kitchen, my mom was just standing there, crying. She didn't say a word the entire time. She just wanted us to be happy, to be a family. That option went out the window when my dad told me to, and I quote, get the hell out of his house.

I turned to my mom when he said that, and I asked if she was really going to let him do this to me. I told her that was it. She had a choice to make. It was either him or me. She could stop him from throwing me out onto the street, or she could stand behind her husband, but she couldn't have both.

She couldn't so much as get a word out through the tears.

That was the last time I saw her. My dad died a couple years after that. I don't remember what I was doing when she'd called to tell me, to beg me to come to the funeral. I do know that I was drunk. I was so blindly angry seeing her name pop up on my phone's screen, I just let it go to voicemail. When I sobered up the next day, I listened to it, but not all the way through.

I didn't go to the funeral.

It was selfish of me. And cruel. She had tried to call me a few times since then, but I never had the balls to pick up.

I dial the number, nervous about what she'll say, or whether she'll even pick up the phone at all.

"Chris," she says, a mix of confusion and panic in her voice that breaks my heart a little bit. Her voice is raspier, older than I remembered it being. "Is everything alright?"

"Yeah, Mom," I say, walking over to my window. The sun is just starting to rise over the buildings. I look at the cityscape, how beautiful it is, this man-made mountain range. "Everything's fine. I just miss you, is all."

"Oh, well that's nice. I miss you as well." There's an awkward pause, the kind of pause that only occurs between family that have grown so far apart the word barely even applies anymore.

"So, I'm gonna be home next weekend. I was wondering if you wanted to maybe get dinner and catch up?" I speak. "On me, of course."

That's the closest I can get to apologizing. At least right now.

"Chris, I would absolutely love that." The joy in her voice is impossible to contain.

I feel like the shittiest son in the whole wide world. I should've done this years ago. "Great. I'll send an Uber to pick you up around five on Saturday?"

"Perfect." She's choking up. And I know I've made the right decision. "Thank you, Chris. I'll see you on Saturday. I love you."

"I love you too, Ma." I hang up.

*   *   *

It's been a few months since the subway incident, and I've really tried to turn shit around. Everything seems to be going perfectly.

I start actually visiting the places I fly to, rather than just sitting around in the motel room getting wasted and screwing any tail I can get my hands on. Each place has a personality of its own, the people, the food, the culture. I never cared about any of that before. My new favorite thing to do is to go to a local museum, learn about the history of these little places out in the middle of nowhere. The locals really love to talk about their hometown, and that's true for everywhere. There's always a story if I'm willing to look for it.

Alice usually comes with me on these little outings. It's nice having someone to experience the world with. We've started getting kind of serious. My mom was a little wary of the age difference, but when I took Alice to go meet her, all that went out the window. She loves her, and who wouldn't? Alice is a ray of freaking sunshine, always looking for the best in people, always willing to give them another shot.

I guess that's why she put up with me in the first place. And how she continues to.

Every time I'm back in the city, my mom and I go to dinner. Her cough's been getting a little bit worse, but I've got the money to help her see a specialist upstate. I tell her about my trips. She loves every second of it, and so do I.

I've stopped drinking for the most part. That's probably been the biggest, most difficult adjustment I've had to make in this whole "turning over a new leaf, finding my path" stuff I'm doing. Especially those first few weeks. I went cold turkey.

I do not recommend it. Alice stayed with me through the sweats and the shivers, the mood swings, the sickness. I couldn't have asked for a better person in my life. We've started talking about maybe moving in together. That's something I'm still a little unsure about because it's all happening too fast, but for her, shit. I'll do anything.

Brendan even noticed the change in me. It was a couple of weeks after the whole subway thing happened, and we were on a flight out West. I'd called out of work for a week to let myself detox and go through all that shit in the comfort of my own home, not some random hotel room where my willpower would give out the second I saw a minibar. So, when I came back to work, I had a whole new air to me—a whole new outlook on life.

We had a conversation on that flight. A real conversation. I think it might've been our first one ever. He's got two kids at home. I asked where their mom was, and he got real quiet for a second, like he was sussing me out to see if this was just a big setup. But he must've seen the sincerity in my eyes, 'cause I really did want to know. He told me she'd died a few years after his youngest child was born, and they live with his parents most of the time.

He wanted to find another job, one that didn't require him to leave so much, but the pilot gig had benefits he wouldn't be able to find anywhere else—not with his skill set. We got dinner that night, and for the first time ever, he laughed at one of my jokes.

When we went to bed that night, I started talking to Alice to try and figure out a way to get him to stay home with his kids. Alice offered to talk to some of the airport managers back in the city. "My dad knows some people there," she explained, "I'll find out if there's an opening in the air traffic control tower." She's brilliant, my Alice.

And we did it. We pulled a few strings, and later that month Brendan was moved from being a pilot over to manning the tower. Never told him I was the one that made the call, but he knew. He thanked me at the celebration/send-off dinner the crew had for him. It's a shame too, I was really starting to like him, but at least he'll be able to see his kids. We go out to dinner at least once a month though, check in on each other.

* * *

Even with all this going on in my life though, I still feel like there is something amiss. There's something deep in my soul that was touched that day in the subway. I've tried everything to get back to that place. I go to therapy. We work on all these kinds of coping mechanisms, so I don't feel the need to go back to drinking and sleeping around. My shrink said that I might have a latent thrill-seeking nature that was activated during that incident. We've been trying to work through it, and I still go see him regularly, but talking shit out never really does it for me. But he definitely got something right.

I need that excitement back in my life, that high of having my blood pounding in my ears, my hair standing on edge, my heart rioting against my ribcage. If I'm not going to drink anymore, I need to get fucked up some other way.

I picked up rafting and mountain climbing. I'm a relatively fit guy, but those were way more effort than they were worth. It didn't really scratch that itch. I started going to a local theme park on the weekends, finding the biggest, fastest freaking roller coaster I could find. That was a little bit closer, but I could only ride them so many times before getting numb to the feeling. I even went so far as to go skydiving!

That was pretty damn close.

The drop in my gut standing on the edge of that plane door; the electric tingle ran from my balls to my toes looking out over the edge. I love feeling the wind against my face as I plummet towards the Earth. Each time I do it, I wait a little bit longer before I pull on the ripcord. The last time I went, the guy they had strapped up on top of me pulled it. He started yelling at me when we landed, saying how irresponsible it was, how close I was to getting us both killed.

At that moment, I felt almost exactly the same as I did on the subway. Even as he was screaming at me, I couldn't get this shit-eating grin off my face.

The company banned me from ever diving with them again. I tried to go back to the theme park, but it's just not the same.

Something is unhinged. It grows with time, gnawing inside. I felt like something was stolen from me, and whatever *that* was, it was what I was looking for.

I've been jonesing for a fix ever since.

*　　*　　*

It's the night of my and Alice's anniversary. I forgot to schedule a reservation. Well, not really. I can't say I forgot. I remember just fine, but we got into a fight earlier in the week. She caught me drinking again. I tried to stay clean for her, but doing things for other people always just ends in resentment.

We've been going on flights separately a lot more often now. She probably requested it. Ever since we moved in together—which was her fucking idea in the first place—she said that we were "spending too much time together," and that we "needed to have separate work lives."

I've got a new co-pilot; his name's Paul. If I thought Brendan was bad, Paul's a million times worse. He can't stop trying to make conversation, and he can't read the room well enough to know that I couldn't give less of a damn about his model plane collection. Not to mention he's only got one joke, and it's about how often he needs to shit. Makes me regret getting Brendan that job. At least he was quiet most of the time.

Now when flying, the second we deplane, I head straight for my hotel room. I empty the minibar, order a couple of drinks from the hotel bar, jerk off, and go to bed. I don't even bother leaving and talking to these dumb hick locals. Once you've seen one small town in the middle of bumblefuck, you've seen them all. They've all got the same story. Someone moved out from a city out East to make it big out West, or the other way round, their wagon broke down in the middle of nowhere, and his inbred descendants are still in the town to this day.

Yee-fucking-haw.

Flying's the only kind of thrill I get anymore. When we hit some turbulence, my heart starts to pound and a smile creeps onto my face that I just can't get rid of. There was a time we dropped a few thousand feet in a blink of an eye. I think about that at least once a day.

But tonight, I'm two glasses into a bottle of scotch, waiting for her to come storming into our apartment. We're going to fight again. We're probably going to break up. I've been trying to make it happen for at least a month now. She's gotten clingy.

I haven't even told her that my mom died. That would just make things worse.

Right on time, I hear keys jingle in the doorway.

The dog we adopted from a shelter together starts barking. I shout at it to shut the fuck up, but that only makes it bark more. It was a mistake to say yes to getting that dog. I don't even like dogs. And it's not fair to the damn thing, it's alone most of the time anyway—though it probably doesn't even realize it since it's so goddamn old.

"Nice of you to finally show up," I say. I take a sip of whiskey and look at my distorted reflection in the bottom of the glass.

And so it begins.

We get into a screaming match, and I'm surprised the neighbors don't call the cops on us.

She starts asking me about Michelle. She's always asking me about Michelle. She thinks I'm cheating on her. It's not like she's the only broad in the whole universe I can hump. I can sleep with anyone I want to.

Fucking women.

"If I was cheating on you," I remark. "It'd be with someone way hotter than Michelle. Though I could fuck Michelle any day of the week, and there's nothing you could do to stop me. She'd be fucking *thrilled*." That part I probably wouldn't have said out loud if I wasn't blasted. I don't necessarily regret it. It's not like it wasn't true.

"Fuck you, Chris," she says. There are tears in her eyes. Part of me wants to go comfort her. To apologize to her and tell her I didn't really mean it.

But that would be a lie.

Eh, she'd probably get over it in a week. She'd stay at her sister's place for a little bit, and I'd come over with a bundle of flowers and chocolates, put on my saddest puppy dog eyes, and say, *I'm sowwy*.

She usually ate that shit up.

Well, to be honest, it's not gonna work this time. Or ever again. Not after today's events.

She heads straight into our bedroom and starts packing up her shit. And I mean, all of it. I'm only three glasses in now, albeit pretty fucking filled glasses, but my tolerance is next to nothing after being sober for so long. I try to stand up, and I fall back to the couch.

"What are you doing?" I slur my words together a bit.

"You don't get to know that," she hisses, carrying a couple of bags out of our room. She grabs the leash that's hanging by the door and grabs the dog, who seems more than content to be going for a walk with her. "I'll be back for the rest of my stuff and Rufus's later in the week. I'll have my sister call you so you can be anywhere else. Goodbye, Chris."

* * *

"And before I can even come up with a coherent response," I tell Brendan the next day at dinner, "she slams the door behind her, and I'm left alone in my apartment."

"I'm really sorry to hear that," Brendan says. "I know how much you two cared about each other."

From the second I walked in the door, Brendan could see something was wrong. I didn't want to talk about it at first. I kept pretending like everything was alright, that I was fine, but he wouldn't give up. Even after I told him to back off it, he wouldn't let it go. So, I just told him so he would get off my back about it.

"Eh, it's alright," I say, finishing off another beer. "Plenty of fish in the sea, right?"

Brendan hesitates for a second. Shitty jazz music plays over the radio of the diner, matching the sound of the rain falling against the concrete outside.

While he's not saying anything, I wave over the waitress, and wink at her. "Hey, doll, could you get me another one?"

She has that fake, cheesy smile waitresses always do when they want to smash a glass over your head. "Absolutely sir, I'll get that for you right away."

I stare at her ass as she walks away. In my mind, I think of all the things I can do to her now that I'm a free man. I turn back to Brendan, who looks more uncomfortable with each passing second. "What? You look like you got something to say."

"Look," he says, steepling his fingers in front of him. I always fucking hated when he did that, trying to make himself look smarter than he is. "You know I'm your friend right? That I care about you, and only want what's best for you?"

I lean back into the seat and cross my arms. "Sure, I guess."

"You really helped my family out by getting me that job in th—"

"Look, B, where are you going with this?" I say, with a little more venom in my voice than I intended.

Brendan takes a deep breath and closes his eyes for a second. My therapist tells me I should do this too, whenever I start getting too worked up. It's called centering, or grounding, or some shit. I try it with him. We must look like two freaks in the middle of this diner.

"You've made a lot of progress," Brendan says after a second. "I'm really proud of the person you've become, Chris. I don't want to see you slide backwards, is all."

Something in my chest ticks, like a time bomb about to go off, but I take another breath and push it down. I hold it off for another day. "I know, B. And I won't, I swear. I'm just in a rough place right now."

"You're welcome to come over to my place anytime you want," Brendan says. "You know that, right?"

"Yeah," I say as the waitress brings the glass back over. Part of me really wants to drink it, but I know I shouldn't. I push the glass away. "I appreciate it."

"Have you talked to your therapist about all of this?" Brendan asks.

"Yeah. He thinks it's all self-sabotage or some shit," I say, unable to take my eyes off the beer. "I don't think so."

"Then what do you think it is?" Brendan looks at me, and then looks down at the glass, and then back at me. "Do you want me to drink that instead?"

I nod, and clench my jaw before I say, "I haven't been the same since that whole thing in the subway."

Brendan grabs the glass and takes a small sip. I've talked about the subway incident with him a couple times. Nothing too in detail. Still, he knows how much it changed me.

"I was riding high off of that for a while," I say. "Shit, it made me change my whole fucking life around. But now it just feels like I'm always chasing that high. And nothing quite hits the spot that same way."

"That makes sense," Brendan utters. "It's just like anything else, the first time is the most intense, and everything after that is just trying to match it. Even though you know it never will. It's a dangerous place to be. Are you still in therapy?"

I nod, distractedly. I start thinking out loud. "There was one time it felt kinda the same, though."

Brendan raises his eyebrow over the rim. My reflection stares back at me from the bottom of the glass. I tell Brendan about the skydiving incident. His eyes get a little wider as I'm talking, but he doesn't say anything.

"That was the closest I've ever gotten." I tap my fingers against the table. "But it still didn't feel exactly the same. Felt like I'd been cheated out of something, honestly." I look back at Brendan's face. He's doing a bad job of trying to hide how horrified he is. "I don't mean I wanted to die or anything like that. I just, I don't know. It sounds fucking crazy, I know."

The waitress brings the check over to Brendan and smiles at him. She doesn't even look in my direction. He grabs it without a second thought.

"Not crazy," he says, pulling his credit card out of his wallet and tucking it in the check. "Definitely a little strange though.

Maybe it's not the adrenaline rush that changed you, then."

"What do you mean?" I can't follow his logic.

"Maybe it has more to do with the old woman than anything else," Brendan continues, sitting up a little straighter. "Maybe it was knowing that you'd actually done something heroic. That you'd risked your own life, to save hers—a complete stranger. That was something I never would've expected out of the old Chris…no offense." He catches himself, grimacing at his unintended insult.

I didn't even notice. I was too busy with a revelation.

"No, you're completely right. I'm a selfish asshole. It's who I've always been," I admit. But that day, after I ran into my old college friend, that's when it all changed. I had that old woman's life in my hands. I could've done nothing, and just let her die right there on the tracks in front of all those people."

"Maybe you should look into being an EMT or something," Brendan suggests as we walk over to the diner counter to pay. "Help you deal with that savior complex of yours."

He laughs, but I can barely even pay attention. A lightbulb has gone off in my head.

Brendan's arm slapping against my shoulder brings me back. "Seriously, Chris, take care of yourself. If you need anything, you know I'm here for you."

"Thanks, B." I try to sound calm. "I've got a redeye tomorrow morning, but I'll definitely reach out when I get back."

"I'm looking forward to it." Brendan smiles as we walk through the front door, into the rain.

*　*　*

It's too fucking early for this flight, and a storm is still raging outside. But we take off anyway. There's a bit of turbulence, but nothing I can't handle. It feels good. My heart skips a beat as the plane bursts through the clouds.

Paul notices how fucking giddy I am.

"Poured a couple extra shots of Jam-O into the old bean juice this morning?" Paul probes.

"Nope," I reply, ignoring the fact he really just said *bean juice*. But I'm in too good a mood for that to bother me right now. "I've just been shown my true path. Everything has aligned like it was done by God Himself."

Paul looks at me, his brows furrowed in a look of pure confusion. "I never took you for a man of faith."

"I'm not," I say.

"Should I be worried?"

"Not at all. Everything's aces."

"Well, either way." Paul literally slaps his knee. "I'm happy for you! It's a beautiful thing when a man finds his way."

I chuckle to myself while Paul collects his thoughts.

"Does this mean you'll come out to dinner with the crew when we land," Paul says. "'Stead of holing yourself up in the hotel room?"

"I think I might," I say, only half lying. "If everyone promises not to be such assholes about it."

Paul rolls his eyes and mutters under his breath, "Sounds more like you."

I ignore him. I'm riding this wave of adrenaline as far as it'll take me. We sit in relative silence for an hour or two. Even though we're flying near the top layer of clouds, the turbulence hasn't gotten much better. The plane's being shaken around like a dog's chew toy, and I am loving every second of it. A flash of lightning cracks, and thunder engulfs the plane. In my suavest, most comforting and confident pilot voice, I make an announcement to the passengers.

"Hey folks, as I'm sure you know, we're experiencing a little bit of turbulence here," I say into the PA system. "Nothing to worry about. I'll get you all to our destination safe and sound. You're in good hands. Thank you for flying with us."

"Well," Paul says, turning to me. "If you've got everything here under control, I'm gonna go hit the little pilot's room."

"It's a free country," I answer.

"Okee doke. I'll be quite a bit though." Paul stands up from his seat, hand draped over his gut. "Had some lamb curry for dinner last night with the old ball and chain at this Indian place uptown. It was impeccable, but my stomach isn't too happy with me at the moment. Sure you're alright?"

"Yeah, sure I'm sure," I say. "I definitely don't want you here making a Dutch oven out of the cockpit. I'll be fine."

Paul does a two-finger salute. Before he leaves, he walks over to the comm system to call in a stewardess to cover him.

"Could you get Michelle in here," I ask, as innocently as I can.

"But isn't Sharon the appointed cover for the flight?" Paul hesitates, his hand hovering over the radio.

I wave my hand at him, trying to override his logic and protocols. "I need to go over the emergency plan with Michelle anyways. I've been flying with her for a decade. Sharon's only been here for like a year."

"Sure, whatever you say, Captain." Paul picks up the radio. I can hear the reluctance in his voice. "Hey Sharon, can you send Michelle into the cockpit. I know, I know, but he says he wants to go over the emergency plan." He puts up the radio and turns back to me. "She'll be right in. Now I've got to go before I make a Jackson Pollock all over this floor."

Paul exits, cackling at his own joke. Michelle enters almost right away.

I've never fully appreciated Michelle's beauty. She's got a refined look to her, I guess, in that MILF-y subordinate way old-school stewardesses tend to have. She closes the door behind her, looking a bit confused, but excited. As if she knows why I really called her in.

"Hey there, sexy." I curl two fingers at her, beckoning her over to my lap. "Come on, I don't bite." I wink at her. "Actually, that's a lie."

Michelle laughs, and it doesn't sound as bad as it used to. Still bad, but I could get over it. She walks over and takes a seat in Paul's chair.

"Suit yourself." I shrug. "So, any plans tonight? Paul invited me to the crew dinner, but I was wondering if you wanted to do something. Just the two of us."

"What about Alice?" Michelle asks.

"Alice and I have been done for a while," I say, sliding one hand onto her thigh. "And besides, it's just you and me in the *cock*pit."

Michelle squirms a bit under my hand. But she doesn't move it away. "Captain, you better behave now."

"And what if I don't?" I gaze at her. "Will you treat me like a bad boy?"

Michelle slides over and sits on my lap. "Is that what you

want me to do?"

"More than anything in the world," I say.

We start going at it. My mouth sucking her face, hands groping and rubbing greedily. It's pure raw passion, like I haven't experienced in months. The storms getting a little bit worse, but who gives a fuck.

Michelle pulls my hand away, bites her lip, and asks. "Do you have any condoms?"

"Don't need one. Got no time for that." I pull her closer. She puts her hands on my chest and shakes her head.

"Seriously? Where's your sense of adventure? It's not like we're strangers," With a wink, I grope her breast. She smacks my hand, wagging a finger.

I sigh. "Fine!" I pull my wallet out of my pocket to check. Nothing. I shake my head. "Nope, you?"

"I think so," she says. "But they're in my carryon back in the cabin."

"Then what are you still doing here? Go grab them, quick! Before Paul gets back here."

"Do we have enough time?" she asks. The rain hits harder against the windows. It sounds like a drum solo of my favorite song.

"He's gonna be a while," I groan. "Trust me, you don't wanna hear the details."

"I don't know," Michelle tilts her head. "We're already breaking so many rules, I don't want to draw any more attention to us." The way she says us, it sounds like she's already planning a wedding in her mind. I'll deal with that later.

"Just pretend that I've got a headache or something, and you're grabbing me aspirin."

"If this costs me my job, you're paying my bills." She squints her eyes at me as she straightens her uniform. She pulls out her phone and turns the camera on. She starts straightening out her hair and makeup. I see myself in the corner of the frame. My eyes burning wild with pure ecstasy.

"Scout's honor." I put my hand over my heart and flash her my best smile. "Now move your cute little ass along and get back in here stat!"

Michelle puts the phone back in her pocket. "Okay, okay, you win."

I turn back in my seat, looking ahead at this torrent coming down on us. Something's about to happen. It's just a sense that you get when you've been doing something as long as I've been flying these planes. If they were smart, we never should've taken off in these conditions.

But I'd insisted everything was fine. And somehow, I'd managed to convince them.

"I'll be back in a jiff," Michelle smirks. "No monkey business, mister."

"None at all." A smile curls on my lips.

Michelle glances back at me one last time before she sticks a wedge under the door behind me.

The second she's out of sight, I rush over to the door, and I try to kick out the wedge. It doesn't budge at first.

Shit. Come on, you stupid fuckin—

On the second try, the wedge goes flying into the cabin. The door slams closed. If I'm going to do this right, I can't have anyone else interrupting me. I want to be able to do this my way.

It's going to happen any second now. I can feel it in my

fucking bones.

I head back to my chair and buckle in. Sweat starts to drip down the side of my face, and it feels good. It reminds me I'm alive. The most alive I've ever been.

Michelle's muffled voice comes from the other side of the door. "Chris. The door's closed, let me in."

I don't respond.

Gentle taps start against the door. Silence.

"Chris!" More frantic knocks. Then footsteps make their way over to the door. More voices. They start banging on the door, trying to get my attention.

The engines slow down as ice starts to form on the blades. I could fix this right now if I wanted to. I could change the angle of the nose. I could rev the engines a bit, spin them faster and get us all out of this. But I don't.

The plane stalls.

For a second, there's nothing but pure silence. This was what it must have been like at the moment of birth and will be at the moment of death. This is the most sacred sound in existence.

My stomach drops, and my arms start to tremble with adrenaline and pleasure. We hold there, in that infinite moment, like a paper plane flown from a skyscraper on a windy day. Then it happens.

We drop.

I hear screams and groans coming from the cabin. There are thuds of objects and bodies crashing against the ceiling. I know how to fix this. All I have to do is tuck the nose down. All I have to do is pick up the engine.

But this feels too good. *This* is the feeling I've been

searching for.

My heart pounds in my throat. The sounds from the cabin get louder. The passengers and crew are crying and begging for God to save them.

But God can't help them now.

Only I can.

The plane continues to drop, and now we've hit the point of zero gravity. Everything just floats.

My phone is hovering in midair. For a fraction of a second, I see a shape in its black screen. The flash of a smile. Like a crack on a shattered mirror.

My hands are on the controls. Jittery as a fleeing, inflamed dragonfly. We continue to drop. Five thousand feet.

Not yet.

Seven thousand. Tingling all over my body.

Just a little bit more.

Ten thousand. My heart is close to bursting.

More...

Mind led body

to the edge of the precipice.

They stared in desire

at the naked abyss.

If you love me, said mind,

take that step into silence.

If you love me, said body,

turn and exist.

— Anne Stevenson

INDEX

THANK YOU

Thank you very much for reading my collection. I truly hope you enjoyed it. If so, please share this book with your friends and family.

Would you please leave a review on your preferred platform(s)? Reviews are especially important for indie authors like me, as they help me reach more readers like you, and in turn, enable me to write and publish more books.

I genuinely appreciate your time and support.

Warmest regards,

Tamel Wino

www.ekleipsis.ca